That Lofty Sky

That Lofty Sky

HENRY BEETLE HOUGH

THE BOOK LEAGUE OF AMERICA

Garden City, N. Y.

PRINTED AT THE *Country Life Press*, GARDEN CITY, N. Y., U. S. A.

CL

For
BETTY

That Lofty Sky

1

ON THAT FATEFUL DAY of the new war there was lying in the harbor of Danzig a gray vessel with guns, representing an older period of naval design but still maintained as a part of the German military establishment. To the ordinary layman this vessel looked formidable enough, but to naval experts and most boys, who have a nice discrimination regarding the models of motorcars, the performance of the newest airplanes, and the capabilities of devices of war in general, her inadequacies must have been apparent. This veteran warship, which was named the *Schleswig-Holstein*, all at once fired a shot into the fortifications of Danzig harbor, and it is said that this was the first shot of the new war which had been almost universally dreaded. The destruction wrought by the opening gun was satisfactory, considering the age of the vessel and her equipment.

The launching of the war was a feather in the cap of all those who manned the *Schleswig-Holstein*, but there was one patriotic young man, once a member of her complement of junior officers, who was not aboard at the time. His name was Hugo Becker, and he had left the vessel in South Africa a number of months earlier.

The *Schleswig-Holstein* had been given over to training cruises for cadet officers and others, and she arrived at Capetown early on a morning in January 1938, long before her part in the new war, which was already being dreaded, had been determined by destiny.

There was a sweetness in the early morning, and a land smell which went with the lofty table top of the mountain stretched out above the city and with the trees and parks which were green and in full leaf in the profusion of the southern summer. The first light was purple and blue, so much so that it was hardly light at all, but more like an effortless wonder of the imagination, and the lamps of the city still glowed and twinkled. The stars in the sky could not be more impressive or beautiful than these twinkling lights of the city giving way in the blue, cool dawn, with the mountain standing majestically above, mighty of mass but delicate and Euclidean of line.

Conditions of sea communication and travel being what they were at that period, which is to say free and safe, the German cruiser was far from being alone in Table Bay. There was an American freighter called the *West Isleta*, her rust concealed under new paint, with a deckload of fine American donkeys embarked through the port of New

Orleans from the plains of Kansas; a gaudy-spirited Italian liner bearing the proud name *Giulio Cesare*, ready to sail with fruit and passengers for Europe; the Dutch freighter *Aagtekerk*, calling for a hundred tons of fuel oil, which was just a commodity at the time and not yet a priority item on war lists; the freighter *Clan Macbrayne* with three hundred tons of mixed cargo to discharge at the South Arm; the *Edinburgh Castle*, in with mail and passengers from Britain, and the Portuguese steamer *Joao Belo*, Lourenco Marques for Lisbon, calling for stores. The Russian tanker *Batoum* had only just sailed, heading around Cape Agulhas to the Indian Ocean and East London.

It was a motley but in a way a glorious international company, and none of the vessels showed the slightest displeasure with the rest. Even the big guns of the *Schleswig-Holstein* and her low, gray, armored hull did not seem particularly sinister. Trailing the cruiser came the tanker, *Schwarzes Meer*, carrying reserve provisions of food and oil, because it was the new rule in Germany to give an adventuring gunboat only a little pocket money, the least amount of cash possible, and to let her buy nothing in foreign ports except lettuce, oranges, and the like. For the most part, the crew of the *Schleswig-Holstein* did with tinned vegetables and dried foods stored in the tanker.

At Capetown, however, there was no dearth of fresh produce, cash or no cash, for the German market gardeners who lived on the flats came crowding to the docks, with their lorries heaped up, their faces broad with welcoming smiles. The arrival of the *Schleswig-Holstein* was a

festive occasion. She flew the swastika from her forward staff, and just below it on the metal of her prow were
the names of the two old duchies from which she took her
name.

While the other vessels transacted their business at the
docks the visiting cruiser discharged parcels of cadets and
young officers into the city to become acquainted there.
They went into the shops of Adderley Street and up the
road to Kloof Nek in order to take the cableway to the
mountain and through the paths of the botanical gardens
near the parliament buildings. They went to Groote Schuur
to sit briefly at the feet of Rhodes, whose classical library
and formalized memory was a puzzle to some of them. First
and last, in the few days the *Schleswig-Holstein* lay in
Table Bay they saw about everything, from the sweet
green vineyards of Constantia to the Cape point itself.

They went into a milk bar here and there and were
greeted by buxom country girls who spoke to them in Afrikaans and laughed with them merrily. There was no lack
of boys and girls of their own people to show them the
sights, and some of them sat in the Waldorf in the evening
and listened to an entertainer burlesquing American radio
programs. In the afternoon many of them had tea at the
Del Monico palm court, served by suave and silent Indians
dressed all in white, and a tremendous amount of it.

The young German named Hugo Becker was one of
these sight-seers and one of the most interested. It would
be a mistake to suppose that the cadets of the *Schleswig-
Holstein* were all round-headed, with heavy, gross features,

or that they went about with leers and a swagger. On the contrary, most of them had rather thin, eager faces and frank eyes. They seemed to be kind, and toward their South African friends they exhibited the greatest modesty and appreciation, blended with a lively curiosity. And their appearance—it was the apotheosis of neatness. Their uniforms of navy blue were precisely fitted and pressed, without a fleck or a mote showing upon them, and the gold thread of the swastikas which some wore upon their sleeves was shiny.

Hugo Becker had fair hair which was neatly brushed, blue eyes set off by his smooth tanned cheeks, lean but not too lean over rather delicately molded cheekbones, and altogether a sensitive, boyish face. His nose was thin, forming a pleasant accent. But his boyish quality was drawn into a somewhat ascetic cast, a kind of trained maturity giving him dignity and breeding along with his inextinguishable youth. Any family might have been proud of a son such as he, but he seemed unaware of himself as a personality, and he was never detached from a group except temporarily. There was only a kind of eager hunger in his eyes as he spoke quietly and laughed quietly with the others. The whole tenor of his conduct was serious and not that of a youngster on a lark, as would certainly have been the case with most American boys under these circumstances.

While the *Schleswig-Holstein* was at Capetown she attracted considerable attention of a favorable sort, and the Germans of the Cape were glad to visit her and to learn something of naval life. Most of the things they learned were true enough, in ordinary course, but some were fanciful. For instance, they were told of a remarkable German naval specialty in the food line, known as "*labskaus*," which was concocted of fish, meat, potatoes, and beetroot, and eaten with pickled cucumbers. The recipe, they were informed, had probably come from one of the eastern provinces of the Reich, but for a long time it had been associated with sailors. Their informants were honestly ignorant of the fact that lobscouse, immemorially, has belonged to the sea and not to any nation.

After a few days a large party of cadets was formed and sent by rail a thousand miles to Johannesburg, for it was thought proper that they should know the interior of the country and see the life of the great city of gold. Hugo Becker was not one of this group and hence did not experience the high air of the Rand or see the white heaps of exhausted sand or the tall modernistic buildings or even walk along Eloff Street, which is one of the fine streets of the world. But in Capetown he had seen the statue of Rhodes looking north.

The visit of the Germans in Johannesburg caused a great furor, and petitions were presented to the mayor asking that these boys be rebuffed and turned away. The newspapers reflected the fulmination, and it was made perfectly clear that the city, officially, was giving no welcome to anyone wearing the swastika or coming from a Reich in which Adolf Hitler ruled. Yet, on the other hand, Johannesburg was formally polite, and there was even some kind of reception at municipal expense, so that no one was really satisfied, whatever his politics.

Hugo Becker, missing all this, nevertheless became one of another expedition from the *Schleswig-Holstein* which was sent to take a look at the Indian Ocean coast. With a party of his comrades he arrived early in January at a town known as Port Quentin, and by a peculiar chance was accommodated at the Beach Court Hotel, belonging to Victor Tolley, which was perhaps the one place in all South Africa where he should never have gone.

2

As the map of africa lies on the page of a book, Port Quentin is perhaps the width of a man's thumb from the lower tip of the continent. It is built close by the mouth of a muddy river which runs into the sea between two rocky portals which the stream itself grooved deeply long ago. Out of the rising bluffs the tree trunks grow from precarious holds, twisting and reaching upward like gray sinews elementally dissected and put on public show. Above the crests the green takes hold in tropical profusion, and it spreads also along the river banks on one of which the road has found barely sufficient width below the rocky walls. In this way the majesty of nature provides for the eye of the European vacationer the distinctly European reward known as a view, and it was predestined from the first that the settlement at the river mouth should become a resort.

The name, Port Quentin, carried certain implications of a commercial character, and they were not intended to be ironic. The river was actually navigable, much of the time, for a distance of about twelve miles, until a cable was strung across for the purpose of a ferry just above the town, and a jetty was built which the inhabitants of Port Quentin hoped sometime might be extended. If it was this the German boys came to look at, they must have been disappointed.

Under the rock escarpments the white people built their two hotels and their cluster of dwellings, all the color of cream or terra cotta. Some of the houses were made large, with terraces and lawns, and others were planned more frugally and kept less neatly. But all the buildings of the town, from the beginning, had one thing in common: their roofs, whether of galvanized iron or tile, were always bright red, so that the whole settlement gleamed like a gay flag when one looked down from the heights above.

There was never any winter in Port Quentin, and the rain could be expected seasonally more than a hundred days in the year.

For five shillings a month a resident of the town could have the public water, which was introduced some years ago from the hills three miles away, and for another five shillings he could be connected with the public system of water-borne sewerage. The rate, or the tax, was always moderate, amounting to about eight dollars a thousand in

American terms, and the municipality found it possible to put up a new town hall. Then the Union government provided a new post office, of the creamiest stucco imaginable, shaped along modernistic lines. There was never any smoke, and dust never spoiled the freshness of the town.

The two hotels, the Beach Court and the Queens, were placed almost side by side, but at an angle, so that only one corner of each approached real neighborliness with the other, and the buildings as a whole spread apart as from a pivot. There was a wide street in between, lined with trees, and in the segment formed by the angular divergence of the buildings was a kind of public square with a rusty old cannon preserved as a monument to a vessel wrecked on the coast long ago. Both hotels were conceived as long stucco structures two stories high, with balconies at the second-story level running almost entirely around them. One turned out cream-colored, and the other a gentle tan, and both had red roofs of corrugated and galvanized iron.

Victor Tolley, a youngish man not much past thirty, came into possession of the Beach Court through the solicitude of his mother, who felt that he should be established in life. Somewhere she found the money to effect a purchase of the hotel, and, in the pleasure of this success, she handed the money to her son, expecting that he would complete the transaction forthwith. This he did, in a way, but not precisely as she had foreseen. Victor, who embodied some but not, by any means, all of the virtues of the British Empire, went to Johannesburg and was tempted. He bought the Beach Court, but, instead of paying for it with cash, he simply made a down payment and hastened to invest the balance of the money in the shares of a rather obscure gold-mining company.

This course was not without some show of reason, for the nations of another hemisphere had done something about their money, and the price of gold was soaring. Old mines, long closed, were reopened, and the city of the Rand flourished beyond its dreams of former days. There was drought on the veld, the high veld and the low, but prosperity rolled on. Gold was brought out of the deep reef, and the light of the metal was reflected in the faces of all South Africa. But, unfortunately, the shares Victor Tolley had bought were slow about paying. At the beginning of 1938 they were nothing more than an expression of hope on fancy paper, and, like hope itself, the shares could not be sold in the open market.

Victor did not worry, because he was not easily bothered. His greatest regret was that he could not at once realize his desire to provide the hotel with an outdoor swimming bath. Of course the ocean was available for bathing, but it was not of much use most of the time, unless one went a considerable distance away, because the river was continually pouring out muddy water and a wrack of dead tree limbs and such stuff which the ocean promptly tossed back upon the shore and ultimately absorbed into itself only slowly and under protest. Since the outdoor swimming bath was out of the question at the moment, Victor resorted to a lesser improvement of another kind.

He had a petrol pump placed just outside the public bar of the Beach Court.

Victor himself enjoyed the small private bar where a glass of beer placed him in an excellent frame of mind and enabled him to think of the future. Seated here with his thoughts, this being an off season at Port Quentin, he was aware of another defect in his life and he took the first steps toward rectifying it by drafting a letter to Nicky Birch. He loved Nicky. He had known her when she was all knees and black cotton stockings in the uniform of the girls' high school in Johannesburg, and his devotion of late had ripened and deepened considerably. The Beach Court Hotel and his own life seemed woefully incomplete without her.

"Dear Nicky," he wrote, "I think you will like living at the Beach Court. It will be a proper job for you, such as you have always wanted, and you do not have to pay any attention to me or make up your mind about me until you feel like it. . . . A good, up-to-date resort hotel ought to have a hostess. This place is nothing like some of the sweller hotels you have seen, but someday it may be. I am planning to contract for an outdoor swimming bath. Meantime the public water has been laid on, and we are not wanting any of the necessities or conveniences either.

"A hostess is part of my idea, to make the guests comfortable and to pour tea in the afternoon. Of course you must not expect too much of the place right away. It needs to grow, and I know it will grow, and as fast as it does I mean to improve it. That is, the business will grow. Port

Quentin has one of the most desirable climates, and it is far away from everything and yet at the same time quite easy to get to by road. You will see for yourself."

There was much more, for Victor never wrote a short letter, but it was all of the same tenor. When Nicky read it she put her fluffy, yellow-brown head upon the bend of her arm and stared at the ceiling. She could almost see Victor, large and a bit awkward, with no physical grace or charm, yet with an ingratiating quality which was strangely persistent and penetrating. He was always anxious to please, and there was a shy coaxing about his smile. Her heart warmed toward him, and it seemed to her that she really ought to look after him. As hostess, too, she would meet all manner of people from far off. . . . She had always wanted a rub, a taste, a feeling of the distant world and its people.

Therefore Nicky, whose full name was Niccoline, and who was still in her middle twenties, packed her things and made the journey to Port Quentin. What she found there was not exactly the realization of her daydream. The scenery was wonderful enough, and the hotel was pleasantly situated, but an outdoor swimming bath could hardly be considered one of the more obvious or immediate needs. It was true that the public water had been laid on, but Nicky did not enthuse over the use Victor had made of it. In order to reach the men's bath and toilet on the second floor it was necessary for any guest to go outdoors and walk the length of the balcony to a slatted door which was, to say the least, not private. The arrangements on the first floor and for the women were hardly more convenient. The fact that the toilets were always backing up and overflowing was less important, because one expected that in a hotel.

The lounge was depressing. The walls were cracked, and the slip covers on the chairs sagged miserably, as well as being faded and worn. The office was bare and meager, with a much scarred and scratched desk and an uncarpeted floor. The furniture in the bedrooms was uncomfortable and, for the most part, unsightly, and the mosquito-netting canopies over the beds were ineffective by reason of rents and holes.

Victor showed Nicky about the premises, pointing out particularly the site of the proposed swimming bath, and she explored a good deal by herself. When she had seen all she wished to see for the time being she stood under the balcony and looked at the earth which seemed baked, although only a little while ago a shower had fallen. The afternoon sun was hot. Then she went into the empty hotel office, toward the stairs, but before she reached them she saw Victor, sitting in the private bar beside a window overlooking the aridity of the back yard. A glass of beer stood on the table at his elbow. It looked hot, not cool.

"Hello, Nicky," he said, glancing up.

"You're a pretty sight," Nicky said.

"I'm sorry if I'm untidy. I've been having quite a busy day, you see."

"But of all places to be sitting! You could enjoy the

beach or a view of the mountains, but instead you coop yourself up like this."

"It's cooler here than in the office," said Victor. "I don't mind it."

Nicky laughed, and her laugh was an avenue of release. She thought him an absurd figure. Despite his comparative youth, he did not look exactly young. His face was lined under and about his eyes, because he was in the habit of screwing them up when he was in thought or when anything unusual happened. His cheeks were pink without being florid, but there was no telling when the distinction might disappear, and his hair was damp and disordered. In his eyes was a truant look, not precisely defensive, but thoughtful and secret. Nicky had always liked his eyes, and they were seldom secret to her.

"Oh, Vic," she said, "you are incurable!"

"Will you have a beer, Nicky?" he asked.

"Not now, thanks."

She turned and went slowly up the stairs, and he watched her vanish. He was rueful. He knew that Nicky was disappointed in the Beach Court and that she would soon be disappointed in him, if she were not already so.

"She thinks I'm not a man of action," Victor said to himself.

Like many men who have a distaste for physical activity, Victor possessed an active mind and was tremendously resourceful intellectually. He had a plan for everything, usually for crises which never occurred, and he knew himself as capable of meeting all sorts of situations. He sighed to think that Nicky did not know this side of him as he knew it himself. He could bring ideas out of his brain more amazingly than a magician could extract strange objects from a hat.

At present he was working on a scheme to get hold of some ready money, both to please Nicky and to meet certain rather pressing obligations. He peered into his glass of beer and found there what seemed a notable solution. South Africa had two leading brands of beer which were its own, and everywhere one went he was confronted with the advertisements of Union beers and Palace beers. Victor was partial to Union beers, and it occurred to him that he could write to the Union Brewery at Capetown and propose that the Beach Court become an exclusive distributor, in recognition of which the brewery would make an investment in the hotel. Such arrangements were not unusual, and there had been no little rivalry between the two breweries in lining up hotel bars throughout the Union.

Victor wrote his letter, and a plausible and beguiling letter it was. As soon as it had gone to the post he felt that things would turn nicely and that without much delay he would be bringing the Beach Court up in the world in a way to please and astonish Nicky. Also, he would be meeting interest payments and installments more punctually than in the past. He felt all the more confident when he received an acknowledgment from the Union Brewery saying that they were sending their Mr. Hickey to inspect his premises and discuss the proposal. Victor would have

preferred their simply sending on the money, but he began
to look forward to Mr. Hickey's visit.

The trouble was that Mr. Hickey appeared in a checked
suit and a shrill tie, and Victor took an instant dislike to
him. Their conferences were held in the private bar, and
it was all Victor could do after the first hour to preserve
the ordinary civilities. In his inspection of the premises—
and he looked into every odd corner—Mr. Hickey naturally
met Nicky Birch and he insisted upon referring to her in his
talks with Victor as a "cute trick," a "good-looking little
gal," or "that nice-looking little thing in a skirt." Victor
himself took some pleasure in looking at Nicky's calf and
ankle, but it filled him with rage that Mr. Hickey should
be so obviously absorbed and fascinated. It soon became
evident that the brewery man was delaying and temporiz-
ing simply because he liked to stay about the Beach Court
and make up to Nicky.

"Now, getting back to business, Mr. Hickey," Victor
would say. "This place has possibilities. We have every
advantage you can think of."

"Port Quentin is pretty hard to get to," Mr. Hickey
would observe with a preoccupied air because of the difficulty of watching that "good-looking little gal" through
the window. "It's a nice scenic spot, right enough, but I
always say give me the railroad. When you're off the railroad you aren't anywhere, now are you?"

Victor knew very well that this was not Mr. Hickey's
considered opinion but that it was an expedient to keep
the conference going on and on. Still, there was nothing

for him to do but to explain again about the highway motor coaches and the post car from Umtata. When he had made this discourse Mr. Hickey deigned to cock an eye at him.

"Oh yes, I suppose you're not so badly fixed. After all, I did get here myself, didn't I? Well, if you don't mind, I think I'll ask the little lady to show me about the town a bit. See you later."

And Victor had to sit and stew while Mr. Hickey strolled off with the girl for whom he was prepared to lay down his life upon the slightest occasion.

When he had a chance he said to her, "I wouldn't be seeing too much of that chap Hickey."

"Why, Vic? I don't see any harm in him. He isn't so crude as he seems at first—and he's not bad fun sometimes, really. Anyway, I thought you were doing business with him?"

"Well, I am," Victor choked out. "I am doing business with him in a way, but I can tell you I don't trust the chap. I don't like the way he looks at you."

This was the situation when Victor opened his mail one memorable morning and found that he had a reservation for fifty cadets of the Imperial German Navy. He could not have been more surprised if he had learned that his hotel was to be visited by fifty Eskimos or fifty Texas cowboys, for he had not read the newspapers closely and knew nothing of the visit of the *Schleswig-Holstein* to Capetown or of the petition of protest in Johannesburg. He sat with the letter in his lap and began to smile. Then he did a little dance around the room.

"Well," he said to himself, "this is something!"

He smiled more broadly still and cast his eyes about the bar, through the door beyond, and everywhere he could see. It seemed to him that the premises were already alive with German officers and that the reputation and the future of the Beach Court were made. It also seemed to him that with such prospects, which he could only believe would lead to more prospects still, he could jolly well do without Mr. Hickey and the Union Brewery.

He had had no time for second thought when Mr. Hickey appeared, hunting for Nicky Birch, as usual.

"Where's my little sweetie?" inquired Mr. Hickey brightly.

"I don't like your tone," Victor told him. "It can't be said you've got much tone, you know, but what you have got I don't like." He smiled at his jest. "Why don't you just be getting on, Mr. Hickey? I may say you've used up your welcome here."

"What?" said Mr. Hickey, unable to believe that he had heard aright, and then, as his senses assured him there was no mistake, "What!"

Victor yawned, elaborately. His urchin look was not appealing to Mr. Hickey.

"Don't try to come it over me," said the brewery man. "I know you need money. You need it the worst way. . . ."

"Not with half the German navy booked here, I don't. I

can get along quite well without you, I'll have you know, and all I ask of you is just to be getting on."

"The cheek, the bloody cheek!" ejaculated Mr. Hickey.

After Mr. Hickey had left on the highway coach Victor bubbled with good nature the rest of the day. He thought that he had never enjoyed himself so hugely. In the afternoon he walked with Nicky to the white sand of the ocean shore. To reach the sand they had to cross a waste of crusty vegetable matter between the skeleton trees and branches brought down by the river, but at last they stood on the curving shore and watched the brown river water come hurling back in the roll of the surf. Then they walked as far as the headland where the lighthouse stood and retraced their steps slowly.

For once Victor felt that he did not have to tell Nicky that he loved her. Surely she must know. There was a perfect understanding between them, and at times she held his arm and looked at him with amusement not unmixed with fondness. She was thinking that the walk was fun, and she wished Victor would get out of the hotel more, and especially out of the private bar.

They were back just in time for tea and had it together, talking and laughing about insignificant things.

It turned out that Victor's elation, tapering off into warm contentment, lasted exactly four days, and then he received a letter canceling the reservations for forty-eight of the German cadets, leaving him with booking for just two. He did not see through this strange reversal at once, but a little thought made it clear that Mr. Hickey and the

Union Brewery had exercised influence in important quarters in Capetown and had managed the substitution of the Queens Hotel for the Beach Court in the itinerary planned for the young gentlemen of the *Schleswig-Holstein*. The only reason that two were to be quartered with Victor was that the Queens could not possibly accommodate the whole number, and only with the utmost stretching and planning could capacity be found for forty-eight. The Beach Court was, perforce, welcome to the overflow, and much good might it do Mr. Tolley.

"The swine!" said Victor to himself, and then, thinking of Mr. Hickey's own language, "The ruddy swine!"

But he said it without violence, for he was compelled to recognize and in a certain way appreciate Mr. Hickey's finesse. He consoled himself with the thought that he could always write to the Palace Brewery and make a proposition in that quarter. For the time being he decided to let things drift and see what might turn up.

Then came the afternoon, and it was a clear and beautiful afternoon when Nicky Birch stood on the Beach Court balcony with her arms on the railing, thinking of nothing in particular, while the highway motor coach came rolling up before the hotel door underneath. The coach door opened, and a young man in a blue uniform stepped to the ground. He had hit his cap against the side of the bus, and he took it off and ran his fingers over his hair. Something made him look up, and there was Nicky smiling at him, for she could not help herself. She had not expected that he would glance up at her. He smiled back, a little uncertainly, and then reached for his bag, but it had already been taken by a black boy named Jacob.

Hugo Becker often wondered afterward why he had not given Jacob a second look, but, as it was, he noticed nobody except the girl on the balcony.

3

THE COACHES bringing the German boys had come down by winding ways around and between the majestic hills from Kokstad, the railhead on the north, and had stopped to discharge most of their burden at the Queens Hotel. The coaches were driven by young Afrikanders, two in the crew of each, and they had fraternized with the Germans, especially at the stops along the way, as at Flagstaff for luncheon and at Lusikisiki for tea. Thus it fell out that the cadet who would otherwise have been quartered at the Beach Court with Hugo Becker took it upon himself to roost with the bus drivers who had their own arrangements. They had the use of the coaches and of a small building near the river.

So far as the German admiralty was concerned, this arrangement made by the young cadet was entirely irregular, but nobody questioned it, because nobody knew anything about it. The officers in charge at the Queens believed that Hugo Becker had a companion at the Beach Court, whereas he had none, but the coach drivers did have one.

There were two other arrivals at the Beach Court that same afternoon, quite unexpectedly, so that Victor was encouraged once more. These two were an English artist and his wife, Eric and Julie Williams, and they came, not from Kokstad, but from Umtata, the nearest railhead on the west.

When Nicky saw Eric and Julie she liked them and envied them, because they were her first clear glimpse of the far-off world. She had always known of the existence of people like them, but she had known few and perhaps none at all. They were the knowledgeable type of English— one must not meet them unless one wanted to be understood —but they were also considerate, keen, mannered, companionable.

Nicky heard Julie say to her husband, "What a queer little run-down place this is!" Which was true, but it made Nicky feel ashamed for Victor.

In the morning Julie was sitting on the balcony, her chair tilted back, and her feet on the rail, smoking a cigarette. Her bare legs, firm and smooth, the skin darkened by sun and weather, were disclosed to the knees and occasionally above. She was younger than Eric, and she had short brown hair with curls which were deftly controlled and hazel eyes. In repose her face could seem remote, and even cold, but it was seldom in complete repose when anyone else was around. She was watching the movements of Jacob, the black boy, who was sweeping the space in front of the hotel, and just then Nicky emerged from her room upon the balcony.

"Hello!" said Julie, and then, "Is that a typical native boy, would you say?"

"No," said Nicky, "Jacob stands out quite by himself, really. Victor—that's Mr. Tolley—says he's never found a boy with his head full of native lore like Jacob or so up to the mark in all their ways."

They looked down at Jacob, who was clad in a heavy blue coat with shreds of old black braid dangling from the front. The buttons were gone, but Jacob had girded himself around the waist with rope. The coattails were allowed to drag about his ankles, for the coat had been intended for a man almost double his size. Jacob swept slowly, with a deliberate manner, and he paused frequently—not, apparently, to look around, but simply to remain immobile. The morning sun was full upon him, and it was already a hot sun, but he lingered there, wrapped in his greatcoat, instead of finishing his work quickly and moving into the neighboring shade. The reason was that Jacob liked the sun.

"Curious!" observed Julie, looking down. And she made mental notes about Jacob as an interesting specimen.

"He's been a lot of places too," said Nicky. "He knows the country."

Nicky went on about her concerns, and after a little while Eric came out, fresh from his tub and shave. He had alert gray eyes, brown hair whitened at the temples, and clear, healthy skin, and so he was the perfect picture of the cultivated Englishman at large.

"That's a queer one, that black boy," Julie said to him. "The girl here—the pretty little one we saw last night—says he's quite up in native wisdom and an authority on the country about here, and all that."

"I shouldn't think it by the look of him," Eric remarked, smiling.

"Nor should I."

Jacob's conduct presently became singular, for the time had almost come for the ringing of the breakfast bell. He made an end of his sweeping, went off somewhere with the broom, and returned with the bell. They watched him conceal himself among the vines at the corner of the hotel building, waiting, and peeping around the corner with slow stealth.

"What on earth is he up to?" said Eric.

Then they saw. A boy appeared in front of the Queens Hotel a short distance away across the square, and he had a bell also. He seemed to look about him, and then he raised his bell in his hand, ready for a downward swing, but before he could make a sound Jacob had stepped forward into plain view, with his bell loudly, triumphantly clanging. The Queens boy showed some signs of chagrin, and Jacob's face was kindled with joy.

"Fancy that!" exclaimed Julie, and she and Eric went down, rather indolently, to breakfast which began, despite all Nicky's pleas to Victor, with stewed fruit. There was

plenty of fresh fruit in season, but Victor was always forgetting. Stewed fruit was easier.

Hugo Becker held the door open for Eric and Julie to
pass, and they returned his slight smile. Nobody spoke.
Hugo had just dashed downstairs and was off to join his
companions in some excursion of the day. He was not
stopping for breakfast.

Still later in the morning Victor Tolley stood in the
bar, looking out at the bright bare earth in the sunlight
with a slow gaze of satisfaction. Across the path of outer
heat and glare, in the line of Victor's vision, moved a large
fly. His eye dwelt upon the fly with much the same idle
contentment with which it fell a moment later upon Jacob
as he passed the doorway wheeling a barrow. The fly was
nothing more than a natural accessory of the world, and
so was the black boy.

Victor drew his cigar in and out between his lips, and
it crossed his mind that Jacob was well settled in life and
that this was the way to handle the native problem. Give
them something to do and let them improve themselves. He
could see Jacob advancing in the course of years to inside
porter and perhaps to waiter, affording a model for other
black boys of the region. As he leaned reflectively upon
the bar he saw the sunlight cut off and the sudden coming
of a shower. The first raindrops brought Eric Williams
under cover, and Victor began telling him all about Jacob
and how the boy had drifted down from nowhere.

"It was when I was having the public water laid on in
the hotel," Victor said, "and I needed another boy. I said

to him, 'Here you, take this shovel and lend a hand, will you?' And he did, and the first thing that came into my mind to call him was Jacob, and Jacob he's been ever since that time.

"You should hear him go on sometimes. I'll be sitting here in the bar of an afternoon, and he and the rest of the boys will be taking their ease in the sun outside in the back court. They can tell stories, but nobody ever touches Jacob. The things he knows! I mean about his own people and about the whole country. He must have traveled a bit to be able to describe the places he can tell about. I'd like to have seen half as much myself."

What Victor said of Jacob was spoken honestly but it was founded largely upon misapprehension, because Victor had rather taken black boys for granted and noticed little about them except that which was forced upon his attention.

In the first place, Jacob came from somewhere in the Transkei, where the great rounded hills billow up toward the heavens and the white clouds billow down toward the round hills until there seems little space between. He was a foundling, a child of nature, and he had never paid so much as a hut tax for the reason that he had never had a hut which was rightfully his own. Technically he was a detribalized native, but he was much more or much less than that, depending on the point of view.

He had no sense of property or truth or discipline in the white man's sense, and although he liked to listen and observe, within limits, something in him kept eluding the purpose and meaning of the white man and his dogmas. When he came to Port Quentin he was barefoot and in tatters, with a smile on his black face and a wide-eyed curiosity which at times approached the supreme inflection of wonder. In this innocence of good nature and this immensity of speculation there must have been the kindling of destiny, for, of all the thousands of black boys in the lofty territories across the Great Kei River, this one child of fortune walked directly and without effort into an identity in the white man's world.

And it was, strangely enough, the white man's world which had meant everything to Jacob. He had been a spiritual as well as a physical foundling, and from infancy he had been shielded from any clear contact with the authentic culture of his own people, first in the household of a trader-missionary and later in the twilight zones of compound and trading station. He had ridden on busses and trains and worked a bit in garages and hotel kitchens, and, altogether, he had acquired less knowledge of his own people and their past than of the white man's present. He had associated with houseboys and others from whom he had assimilated much excellent English and he had a predilection for such phrases as "you see," "jolly good," and even "a spot of tea," delivered with the proper colonial accent.

What Victor Tolley had taken for a remarkable store of native wisdom was, in fact, something entirely different. The territories which lay behind Port Quentin were without benefit of movie theaters, that modern institution which is known in South Africa as the bioscope. But from time to time a portable bioscope, complete with sound, was taken from settlement to settlement to give performances under whatever auspices there might be, and it chanced that Jacob had fallen in with the bioscope company and witnessed, clandestinely, a showing of one of the most florid and spectacular of the Tarzan films. Greatly amazed and impressed, he had followed the company about as best he could and had discovered that the same wonders were to be seen twice, or three times, or even more, if he was lucky enough to find a place where he could look on. Sometimes when he could not actually see the picture he could hear the sound effects, which were quite worth while by themselves. This experience, or series of experiences, had given him the basis for stories such as no other black boy had ever told.

Victor could hardly have recognized in Jacob's interpretations and elaborations of the subject matter of the Tarzan picture any of their actual derivation. Not even the author or the actors in the picture would have recognized what Jacob's imagination and peculiar genius had done with their creation.

Ultimately, of course, Jacob and the bioscope had parted company, and he had come to the knife edges of rock where he could look down upon the red roofs of Port Quentin at the river mouth. The red roofs in the sunlight had trolled him to his career, and within no very long period of time Victor Tolley had taken him for a wise man among his own people.

And now the shower was over. Eric and Victor saw Jacob pass the doorway in the recurring sunlight, against a background of road which had been made wet-tawny instead of dry-tawny. The boy's face was shiny with the heat, but his greatcoat was wrapped tightly around his slender body. He was smiling.

Eric stepped out into the fresh air. Julie and Nicky were coming toward him across the square. Hugo Becker was off in the hills with his companions, and not yet had the little group at the Beach Court been gathered intimately, within four walls, to face one another and to talk.

4

WHEN HUGO BECKER came in late that night Eric and Julie were sitting in the lounge in front of the radio, listening to the British Empire broadcast. There were new and more terrible bombings in Spain, two British ships sunk in the Mediterranean, a massacre by the conquerors of Ethiopia, sweeping advances by the Japanese in China. Hugo started up the stairs, but then paused for a moment or two, because he caught the sound of Big Ben, and the notes of a great bell are always arresting. It seems to say more than it does, but what it does say is stirring.

"There it is," said Eric.

They had been listening for it. The measured striking of the bell went on, and the vibrations died away on air none of these three had breathed, and yet upon this languid air of Port Quentin too. At the final stroke of the hour the

bell ceased. Time had struck in London. Time had struck
half the world away in the raw January fog. Eric reached
over and switched off the radio, then puffed silently upon
his pipe. Hugo had gone on his way upstairs.

"You don't hear any good news over the wireless these
days, do you?" said Julie in a queer, strained voice.

"We're lucky to be out of it for a bit," said Eric.

"Are we out of it?" asked Julie.

"No, I suppose not, really. We're lucky, all the same."
They did not say anything more.

One thing about Port Quentin was that, season for season, each morning was almost like all other mornings, and
even at this period of rains there might be sun when one
tumbled out, and if there was not there would be hope of
quick clearing. Sun and rain worked in short shifts and
tried to set one another at naught.

The next morning began with sun. Nicky Birch was out
of bed at seven o'clock, the door of her room flung wide
upon the balcony, to let in the cool air before it was too
late. She stood for a while looking across at the green of the
trees on the opposite side of the square and at the brown
sea which lay beyond the beach. Far out a freighter was
steaming up the coast. She watched it out of sight behind
the tall north bluff. Then she turned, ran her fingers through
her hair, and looked into the mirror.

Her face was not so thin as she would have liked it. Her
cheeks were inclined to be round, and she thought her
nose was too snubby. It was a young, mobile face, with
blue-gray eyes which changed expression many times in

response to Nicky's fluid thoughts. She sighed, not from discontent, but because of the general perplexity of life.

This was a morning upon which she was glad to do her exercises, which were entirely self-prescribed. She did them to keep fit, but when she felt stale and cross she did not care whether she was fit or not. When she felt fine she went through each maneuver with gusto, fancying herself more crisp and youthful with every bend forward and back, every sway from the hips, and every lift of the legs.

She was standing in front of the doorway, with nothing on but brassière and panties, arms akimbo, lifting each leg in turn, and putting it down again firmly to feel the muscles tighten under her skin. The air felt pleasant against her skin. She had stood so on many mornings, and there was no reason why she should not, since she had the last room on that side of the hotel and her privacy was complete. But this morning she was startled to hear footsteps, and they did not stop—they came on, not rapidly, but deliberately. She stood teetering, and, to her consternation, Hugo Becker walked along the balcony in front of the open doorway.

Nicky stepped back quickly, too quickly, because she had not reckoned on the chair immediately behind her. The chair went over with a crash, and she went backward over the chair, her legs waving, the rest of her more or less tangled in articles of clothing which had been draped over the chair back. She uttered a sudden cry of alarm and surprise.

Hugo Becker had arisen in good spirits also. He liked this new world because it was completely different from anything he had known. Everywhere he looked he found some virgin quality which puzzled him. If this country was old, it gave no sign of age. It cried aloud for organization and use, but there was nothing imperative about this cry— on the contrary, Hugo found a delicious sense of roominess in time as well as roominess in space. It did not make much difference here whether something was done today or tomorrow. How different from the feeling of life at home! He could see how the new lands must have been to the pioneers.

He wanted a warm tub, and he put on his bathrobe and stepped out upon the balcony to make his way to the slatted door. The air was still cool, although not so cool as it had been the evening before, and he knew from the appearance of the sun that the day would be hot. He noticed a breeze moving the leaves of the trees beyond the square, and his eyes followed farther off to the freighter. He supposed she was British but he could not be sure. There was a shimmer in the air, and the moving hull was not at all clear.

He was not exactly certain now whether he had turned the right way on the balcony or not. He had emerged through his own doorway instead of by way of the hall and the hall passage to the balcony, and there were some rocking chairs which seemed to have been moved recently. He frowned and hesitated and then walked along to see whether he was heading for the slatted door or whether he would have to retrace his steps.

The crash of Nicky's chair and her sudden cry took him completely by surprise, and as he wheeled about he started instinctively to answer the call of distress. He stepped quickly through the door, ready to do what he could for someone who was milling helplessly about the floor. His hand was stretched out, but his fingers slipped over smooth bare skin, and a small silk thing came away in them, and then he realized the truth of the situation. A girl, scantily clad, if she was clad at all, was rolling over and over, away from him, her head buried in a confused mass of clothing.

Hugo darted out of the room and back along the balcony, his neck and face blushing deeply. The small thing of silk he had dropped at once, as if the touch of it had electrified his fingers. He finished his progress toward the bathroom in a sprint and banged the slatted door after him.

The official schedule for this day was a lenient one, and Hugo was supposed to breakfast at the Beach Court. He felt some reluctance to do so, under the circumstances, but it was not in his nature to go back on an official arrangement simply because of his personal feelings. Walking somewhat stiffly, he made his way to the dining room at the first sound of the bell and seated himself formally at his small table against the wall.

Eric and Julie appeared almost at once, and Julie stared at Hugo and nodded with the suggestion of a smile, immediately turning her head away. But although she diverted her gaze whenever Hugo was looking in her direction Julie continued to study him carefully all the rest of the time,

and of this surveillance he was quickly aware. He felt himself coloring again.

"So she was the one!" he said inwardly.

The English, he said to himself, were certainly a strange
people, and, although he could admire English coolness
and calculation in many situations, he was horrified to find
these qualities in a married woman who had been so recently surprised in an undressed state by a stranger.

Julie was studying Hugo because she was interested in
his ideology. Like Jacob, the black boy, he was a specimen,
and she was trying to penetrate some of the secrets of a
young Nazi. She noticed that he seemed to squirm a little,
and she wondered if all Germans had guilty consciences.
She could not possibly know that he was preoccupied with
a vision of two comely brown legs which he conceived to
be hers. He retained no impression whatever of a girl's
face in the balcony room that morning or the color of a
girl's hair, but the legs were in his mind indelibly. Two
waving, thrashing bare legs, flaunting not only the distress
of their owner but also a youth and loveliness of their own.
Hugo peered into his water glass, because he was afraid to
peer anywhere else.

"Isn't that a puzzling thing for you?" Julie observed to
Eric. "I believe that German boy can't bear to look at me."

Hugo was thinking, "How sophisticated she is! How far
from being truly modest."

Nicky came into the dining room a little late, hoping
that Hugo would not be there. She was unjustifiedly angry
when she saw him, but this feeling disappeared when she

found, to her relief, that he did not so much as glance in her direction. He was, in fact, so completely absorbed in attempting to carry off the situation with Julie that he did not think of anyone else. Nicky breathed more easily, and as the minutes ticked on she felt grateful to Hugo for what she took to be his delicacy.

She had been building a wall against him in her own mind, but her feeling of his consideration was so reassuring that the wall was toppled. There in the dining room, over the stewed fruit and kidneys, the awkward experience of the morning was, so far as she was concerned, liquidated. She was sure that Hugo would never indicate by word or expression that he had embarrassed her—and himself—early that day, and this assurance restored her sense of naturalness.

"What a nice boy he is!" she said to herself. "He looks as if he felt perfectly miserable, and it's really my fault."

She looked after him sympathetically as he made a precipitate escape from the dining room. Eric and Julie Williams went out a few minutes later, and no one was left except Nicky and George Parrish, a boy who worked in the Port Quentin branch of Barclay's Bank (Dominion and Overseas) and took most of his meals at the hotel. Nicky lingered over her breakfast, following it with a cigarette. She eyed the ugliness of the stamped iron ceiling and the cracks in the walls, not thinking of them at all, but of vague, immaterial things. Finally she snubbed her cigarette end in a saucer and went forth to meet the procedure of the day, wondering what it would be, since a hostess seemed to have little to do at the Beach Court.

Victor called to her from the office, where he was standing in conversation with Hugo.

"I tell you what would be a kind deed, Nicky, if you're up to a turn about outdoors," Victor said. "This young lad is on his own today, and it's a pity for him to be wasting his time when he's not likely to come this way again for a long while. You could show him around and tell him a bit relating to the locality, you know. Mr. and Mrs. Williams are off to see Mlengana Rock, and I suggested he go along with them—they would have been glad to have one more in the car—but he says he's seen the rock."

"Oh yes," said Hugo hastily. "The rock. I have seen it. Yesterday."

"I'd be glad to take you about," Nicky said to Hugo, "though I don't know that I can give you a proper tour."

"I thank you very much," Hugo said, "but I am afraid that would be an imposition. It was arranged that I should take a walk with my friend Kurt Schaefer, who is lodging with the coach drivers, but they have persuaded him to change his plans."

Hugo spoke almost faultless English—in fact, his English was so nearly faultless that it suggested a synthetic language spoken by a mechanical man. He had almost no accent— just a tendency to make the "v" sound a little like an "f" sometimes. Spoken words usually carry with them some of the soil which sustains the human beings who utter them, and language in general, when it leaves the tongue, has a strong admixture of tradition and environment. Hugo's English had none. Nicky liked to hear him speak, because he sounded so odd and because he behaved with such modesty and simplicity.

"It won't be an imposition at all, really," she said. "Shall we start soon? I can meet you here in twenty minutes."

"This will be a pleasure I had not expected," said Hugo.

Before she went upstairs Nicky said to Victor, "Stewed fruit again this morning!"

"It's hard to get fresh fruit at this time of year," replied Victor mechanically.

Unfortunately for the credibility of his statement, at that particular moment Jacob, the black boy, strolled slowly across the square with a large and succulent bunch of grapes from which he was eating with every sign of pleasure. Nicky glared at Victor, but he merely shrugged.

The sun was not yet too hot for walking of a leisurely sort when Nicky and Hugo started along the road to the lighthouse. In an open field back of the post office a group of native prisoners clad in scarlet jerkins were squatting while they cut the grass with sickles. Two natives armed with guns stood over them. Each boy in scarlet would take a bunch of grass at the top with his fingers and chop it off at the bottom with a sickle. The process seemed impossibly slow.

"There is no hurry here," observed Hugo. "Everyone and everything has plenty of time."

"You sound as if you did not approve."

"It is just that I am not used to this condition. You see, at home there is not time enough to do what must be done."

The surf beat noisily against the shore, not with any special fury but with tireless strength. The air was still and bright. They walked along in silence. Nicky felt at ease with Hugo, except that she was supposed to be a guide and she did not know how a guide was supposed to act. She should, undoubtedly, be giving him some information about Port Quentin.

"The town is on the Umzimvubu River," she said. "That means—at least, so Victor says, and he isn't always right about things—'the home of the hippo.' Not that there are any hippos around now, of course."

"Hippo?" said Hugo uncertainly. "Hippo?"

"I mean the hippopotamus."

"Oh yes! I have seen him in the Tiergarten."

"They tell about Hubert the Hippo," said Nicky. "He spent many weeks in the haunts of his forefathers, but his name had to be changed to Huberta when they found out that he was really a lady. Huberta traveled all through Pondoland, wallowing in one river after another, and a legend grew up among the natives that she was the reincarnation of the chief of the Zulus, Dingaan, and that she had come to bring news that the white man's rule was at an end. A farmer shot her because she damaged his crops, although I daresay she never meant to do that, and when she died the legend died too."

"That is a very interesting story," said Hugo.

"But I always feel sorry for Huberta," said Nicky.

"It is too bad she was shot."

The road wound upward, and soon they paused for a rest and to look back over the way they had come. They leaned against a rock as they surveyed Port Quentin.

"Don't you like the red roofs?" asked Nicky.

"Yes. We have some red roofs at home in Düsseldorf."

"Oh, do you come from Düsseldorf? That is where Heine was born, isn't it?"

"Who?"

"Heine, the poet—*Du Bist wie eine Blume.*"

"Oh! Yes, I believe it is. I had forgotten."

"How funny!" exclaimed Nicky, laughing. "Once I wrote an essay about Heine, and I know something about him that you had forgotten, even though you are from Düsseldorf yourself."

"But Heine was not a real German, you know. We do not learn about him in the schools at home any more, and no one reads his books."

This served to remind Nicky of some of the things she had read about the new Germany, and she said nothing more. They walked on again in silence.

After a while Nicky asked, "You are not angry with me for bringing up Heine, are you?"

"Certainly not. You are being very kind to me. But do you mind if I say that some of the English I cannot seem to understand?"

"I don't know many of the real English," said Nicky. "I'm really a South African myself, though my grandparents came from Devon. There was a plan to send me to school in England, but it never came to anything."

"That Mrs. Williams at the hotel," said Hugo. "She seems so—so cold—so brazen."

"Oh, that's just her way. She's awfully nice."

"Perhaps," said Hugo, "but I do not understand."

The next time they stopped they were higher still, more than halfway to the lighthouse which stood upon an eminence at the tip of the craggy point. The town was smaller now, and they could see it in relation to the river and the towering bluffs. Their eyes followed the whole crescent of white sand and traced the fluid line where the brown met the blue in the ocean. The beauty of the sky and its white clouds was not lost upon them. Without exchanging any words, they sat down among the bushes at the edge of the road and gazed into the distance, and Nicky saw everything anew, because she was looking partly with his eyes.

"It is very strange to be here with you," said Hugo. "You are like an old friend, yet you are the one new friend I have found in a very great while. I had never thought of it that way before, but the life I have lived has kept me all the time with my own people."

"I like being with you," said Nicky, because she did, and it seemed natural to say so.

He changed his position, and his hand touched hers. The touch was accidental, but it meant something to both of them in assurance and understanding. Hugo leaned upon one elbow, and his young profile seemed to invite the sea breeze and the sun. His eyes were serious but so welled up with eagerness and a certain longing that Nicky felt these things strongly. They both sat back where they were shaded from the direct sun, but the light found a way to Nicky's hair and made it glow.

"A day like this comes as a surprise," said Hugo. "Most things you know about before they arrive upon you. You plan and you work, and all things are arranged. But today was not arranged; it just happened, and it is like nothing one ever thought of."

"Don't you go walking with girls in Düsseldorf?"

He smiled and said, "That is different. Yellow pigtails— that is what I think of when you speak of walking with girls in Düsseldorf."

"Well, what is wrong with yellow pigtails?"

"Nothing is wrong with them. They are very nice. But they are not like this, Miss Nicky. They make you think of when you were a small boy, of yellow soap and scouring, of everything which everyone does, of what is planned and expected. . . . Oh, but I cannot explain. I cannot make you see what I mean."

"Yes, you have already explained," said Nicky. "I do understand."

"Then today is something different for you also?"

"Perhaps it is. But don't you think we are wasting our time? I am your guide, and I have shown you nothing yet."

"No. We are making the best use of our time. After all, from here we can see everything."

"We can see just one view of the town in the distance," said Nicky.

"That is not what I mean. What are rooftops and streets and houses, or even the trees and mountains?"

"Well, what more do you see?"

"I wish I could tell you, but I am not sure myself."

He took her hand and held it, as if he needed help. They did not know how much time went by.

Finally Hugo said, "Perhaps I am foolish. Perhaps I cannot see anything at all."

Nicky lay back on a grassy place beside him, and his serious blue eyes looked into her face.

He said, slowly and thoughtfully, "Perhaps I have been looking in the wrong direction. Perhaps I should look into your eyes."

"What do you expect to see there?" she asked, smiling curiously at his earnestness.

"I am afraid, Miss Nicky," he said, "that I am going to make love to you."

"But we are strangers, Hugo, just strangers."

"Please do not speak of that. After all, anyone can see farther and better when he beholds a new view, like this one. It is the same when I look into your eyes, my new young friend. I am glad we have not known one another since childhood—though I admit I feel now that I have missed you."

"You're so serious!" Nicky protested.

"Today is so unexpected and so short. How can I make a light thing of it?"

Her face became serious, too, and he put his arms about her and kissed her. They sat close together, and neither spoke for a long time.

5

Hugo and nicky stood under the balcony of the Beach Court and felt the welcome coolness of the evening air and smelled a certain sweetness which came from the green riverbanks and across the square.

"There is not much time left," Hugo said.

"I never knew that time could go so fast."

"Perhaps it will not go so fast again. I am afraid it will creep very slowly."

"What will happen if you just stay here and don't go to join the others?"

"I am supposed to report to my commanding officer this evening. If I do not go I shall be sent for. That would not be very nice, would it, to be led by the ear, almost, like a little boy?"

"Just the same . . ." said Nicky.

Hugo laughed and said, "There isn't any 'just the same.'"

They were standing in front of the open doors which led into the hotel lounge, and at the sound of voices they turned and glanced inward. All the others were in the lounge, talking and occasionally laughing. Victor Tolley sat in a chair with a disordered slip cover, a leg over one of the arms, taking his ease. Julie and Eric Williams occupied wicker chairs near the center of the room, and Julie was flung down without any attention to form, her legs crossed and stretched out before her, her hands in the pockets of a tweed skirt. George Parrish, the boy from Barclay's Bank, was on hand also, smoking a pipe. His chair was so low that his knees came up in front of him like some unaccountable, useless objects.

The lounge was not a large room, and it was even more circumscribed than it would have been otherwise because of the plethora of useless furniture—three squirmy-legged tables, one with an oversize lamp, and two with vases of dried flowers, and two show-window chairs containing puffy pillows upon which no one with human sensibilities would ever have sat. Yet the atmosphere had a kind of intimacy, and the light was too dim to reach into the corners, so that the hardness of the walls underwent a softening.

"That Englishwoman seems to be making a speech," said Hugo. "I am glad we are out here. These last precious minutes——"

"Don't talk of the shortness of the time," said Nicky.

"Forgive me, I should not have done so, but it almost makes me ache."

Julie was addressing herself particularly to George Parrish, because he was as English as she, and he had not seen Mlengana Rock.

"It's more than a rock," she said. "It's a mountain. You start from here and you go up and up the road through the rolling hills. They're like green velvet. I don't think I've ever seen anything more beautiful than those great, easy, round hills are in their own way. They're so majestic and yet friendly, and there's nothing forbidding or aloof about them. Yes, the whole countryside is as pastoral as an English meadow, if you know what I mean, but pastoral in a vast, roomy, airy way, up against the sky almost. And it doesn't put you in a mood for the rock when you finally come upon it."

"I see what you mean," said George Parrish.

But Eric said, "What's got into you, old girl? You're making a speech."

"I'm thinking about the rock. I wish I hadn't seen it, I think.

"Finally you get to a place where the narrow road is cut into the side of a hill, and the hill turns into a mountain before you expect it. Up and up you go on that steep shelf of a road, and you think the ascent is going to stop just as all the other ascents have, but it doesn't stop. It goes on, until it almost takes your breath. You are on earth, but you are above the earth, and if you dare to look down you see the valley winding away between the smooth velvet hills, and there are villages, native villages, and cattle and a little silver thread of a river down there, so far down and so far off that it is another world. And still the ascent continues. Up and up you go, as if to the rooftop of all.

"Then you see the rock. You have caught one glimpse of it before, but now you see it for the first time for what it really is, and you haven't been prepared. It isn't an ordinary mountain or an ordinary rock at all. It's something architectural. It's a Cyclopean cylinder which rises up like a tower, and its sides are the only bare rock you have seen or will see in the green world all about you. Its top is just slightly domed and covered with green velvet like all the hills of the region. What a mighty, towering thing that cylinder is! How can it help taking hold of your imagination?"

Julie was almost breathless, but she could not stop. She had to explain, to instruct, and she was no longer aware of the presence of the surroundings of the Beach Court.

"They say that in the olden times the cowards and miscreants of the native tribes used to be taken to the top of the rock and thrown into the valley below. Well, I suppose that's not so much, is it? Cowards and miscreants—one doesn't find much pity or consideration for them. But they say that once, and perhaps more than once, a great native chief commanded entire regiments of his finest warriors to leap from the rock, just to show his authority, to prove that they would obey. These regiments leaped, in ordered ranks, yelling out their war cries, charging into space, into the empty air. Can you see them leap and fall? When I was there at the mountain today it seemed as if I could see nothing else."

Victor Tolley gave a short exclamation. He had not been in a mood for horror, but he could not resist the insistence of Julie's words and her suppressed excitement which seemed a kind of delirium. The effect was greater because Julie had not yet fully explained what it was which possessed her.

Both Victor and Eric knew Mlengana Rock, and they were seeing it again, clearly. How far the summit towered above the valley seemed impossible to describe. The height made a gasping distance, a span so great, so sudden, and so unbroken that the eye could not measure it without excitement and awe. They could all see now the regiments of elated, death-stricken warriors charging from the rock, not upon any real enemy, but only upon the clear, sunny air, and then the swift yet lingering cascade of bodies through the immensity of the fall—lingering because from this summit no fall could be over quickly. Then death on the floor of the valley, on the green floor among the grazing cattle, near the silver ribbon of a river flowing so far away.

"Oh well," said Julie, letting her voice drop, "why worry about it? That sort of thing was all over a long time ago. Nobody commands any regiments to go jumping off now, and nobody will."

She spoke as if she did not mean what she said, and the others waited in silence.

"But perhaps it isn't all over. . . . Perhaps we have the same situation on a bigger scale in Europe. . . . Rulers who control whole nations, whole peoples, as absolutely as that native chief controlled his regiments, and these peoples—won't they obey an arbitrary order for mass extinction as readily as any natives ever threw themselves from the rock? Won't they, just! And drag the world down with them, for all we know. Oh, what horror I have of the absolutism which breeds obedience and death, death and obedience, as if for their own sake!

"Instead of a native chief a Hitler, a Mussolini . . . the leadership principle . . ."

Julie looked up just then, as if something told her to look up. Hugo Becker was standing in the doorway in his neat blue uniform with the gold-threaded swastika upon his arm. Nicky was at his side.

"Oh, come now!" ejaculated Victor Tolley suddenly. "Don't let's talk politics!" But he spoke too late.

Hugo and Nicky had been standing outside all the while, and once or twice they had looked into the lounge and seen Julie's lips moving, her face animated with an expression which showed how important her subject was to her.

"What do you suppose it is all about?" Hugo asked once.

"Something grim," said Nicky, laughing. "Don't bother. We are better off out here where we can see and not hear any sad or awful things."

"I have a strange feeling about that woman," said Hugo. "I wonder if I am afraid of her?"

"But why?" asked Nicky. "Just because she's English——"

"No, not because she is English. Something that happened this morning, and the way she looks at me—hard, like this!"

"What a face! She doesn't look anything like that. Anyway, I don't see what could have happened."

"Sometime perhaps I can tell you. Oh, but I keep forgetting that this is the only sometime for us. The minutes are so short and so few."

He held her hand, and they faced about and gazed into the darkness across the square where the shapes of the trees rose against the starlit sky.

Finally Nicky said, "Let me walk with you when you go to take your place with the rest. I promise you none of your friends will see me. I will disappear in the darkness when we are almost there."

"I must make myself ready," said Hugo, "and then we will go. What! She is still talking. I hope she is not talking in such a way about me."

He started to lead the way, through the lounge, but just inside the doorway he paused, and Nicky came up beside him. They both heard what Julie was saying.

"No politics!" cried Victor Tolley again.

Nicky heard a little sound, and even in the tension of that moment she realized that this was the sound made by Hugo's heels clicking together. His body was erect and rigid.

"It is easy for you to make free with the name of the leader of another nation, madam," Hugo said, his voice tight and clipped. "It is easy for you, with the ease and luxury you and your country have enjoyed at the expense of others! Yes, it is easy. It is a very fine thing. It is what we Germans expect from England—lies and black names and misrepresentation. I think that is the correct word, madam.

"What can you know of the leadership principle? For shame! The variety of woman you are——"

"Hugo!" said Nicky, catching his arm. "Hugo!"

He stopped suddenly and strode through the lounge and out the other door, in the direction of the stairs. Nicky ran after him.

"What did he mean by that?—the 'variety of woman' I am—what could he have meant?" said Julie slowly.

Eric was staring after Hugo in an attitude of indecision, but he turned quickly and said, "The boy is off balance. He'll be sorry presently. I wonder how much he heard."

"A good deal, I should judge," said George Parrish. "I suppose all those Germans are like that underneath."

"Not very nice, though, my boy, to hear your god put up against a black native chief," Eric remarked.

"I wish I knew what variety of woman he thinks I am," said Julie, her eyes staring with surprise. "Of course he resented what I said. I did not know he was there. But what a strange thing for him to say to me!"

Victor Tolley had followed Hugo and Nicky almost at once. They had not gone upstairs, after all, but were standing in the hotel office near the main entrance.

It was at the foot of the stairs that Nicky caught Hugo and took his arm so that he could not shake her off.

"You are wrong to be so violent, Hugo," she said to him. "You must not take it like this. What does it matter what things are said? They cannot really hurt you. Hugo, you are to go so soon. I cannot bear to see you like this."

"I could not help it. I could not help it," Hugo said. "When I heard what that woman was saying——"

Nicky led him toward the door.

"You were wrong to lose your temper with her though. You see that, don't you?"

It was then that Victor Tolley joined them, in haste.

"Here you are, old boy," said Victor. "Now listen to just a word or two of wisdom, will you, like a good chap?"

"I was wrong," said Hugo, more quietly, but still in a tense voice. "I was wrong." He looked at Victor as he patted Nicky's arm and said, "She is right, quite right."

He meant that Nicky was right, that he should not have lost his temper, but Victor did not understand. He thought Hugo was saying that Julie was right.

"Of course I'm right," said Nicky, but Victor did not hear her at all, because he was staring, dumfounded, at Hugo.

"Where are you off to now?" Victor asked.

"Oh, don't bother, Vic. Do go back—at once!"

"This may be serious," said Victor excitedly. "Don't go barging off now. Stop a bit and think this over. It wants some thinking, you know."

He had taken Hugo's arm, and Hugo threw off his grasp. He took Hugo's arm again, and this time Hugo pushed him roughly, and he fell over backward into a flimsy chair which collapsed under him and let him down, sprawling, upon the floor like a crab upside down. When he was on his feet again both Hugo and Nicky had disappeared. He rushed out of doors and stood under the balcony, calling after them, but there was no reply, and he did not know which turn they had taken.

Victor returned to the lounge, brushing himself off, for the floor of the hotel office was dusty.

"What was that confounded crash?" asked Eric. "I was on the point of coming to inquire, but it seemed after what has happened that our little group here might conduct itself rather more delicately than usual."

"He did a bolt!" said Victor.

"Who?—the German?" asked George Parrish.

"Who else?" returned Victor, not too amiably. "Let me tell you why he got the wind up, if you can believe it."

"Well, why?" asked Eric.

"Your wife here converted him," said Victor. "His very words to me were, 'I was wrong. She is right, quite right.' I could hardly believe it, but those are the words he spoke. The heat had gone out of him, and he was quite limplike."

"What! Are you sure?" Julie demanded.

"It's not possible," said Eric. "Why, those lads are brought up to believe in Hitler and all his works as we are taught the faith of Christ!"

"But, after all," said Julie, trying to accustom herself to the idea, groping, "he saw Mlengana Rock too. Perhaps the same thing had occurred to him. . . . He's young, and he must have a mind, you know—even a bit of imagination, for it can't all have been trained out so soon."

"Whatever may lie back of it, converted he is," said

Victor, "because that is what he said to me, and it brooks of no doubt. His language was foursquare and flat-footed. I tried to stop him from bolting, but he gave me a blow in the chest, and I went down like a cabbage. What a thing! He's turned against his own kind, that's what it means. His time is about up, too, and soon he'll be missed, and they'll hunt him down and shoot him as a deserter, if nothing worse."

"No, no!" Julie said.

"Why not?" asked Victor. "Mr. Hitler's officers don't take kindly to a change of political views, nor to a breach of orders either. They'll have it out of him what it's all about—you can be sure of that."

"I am afraid you may be right," said Eric.

"We must get hold of him and bring him back," Victor declared. "That's the only way. If he can slip into his place, and no questions asked, he'll be safe. Perhaps he'll get reconverted, and that will be best for him, don't you think?"

Julie had gone to the door and was peering out, but it was impossible to see much. She could discern more in the sky than on the dark earth.

"Very well," said Eric, "we'll get him back."

"I'll have a look about," said Victor.

"So will I," said George Parrish.

The two went out of doors and separated, taking different directions.

"You did preach a sermon tonight, didn't you, old girl?" Eric remarked.

"Yes, didn't I!" Julie was still at the door.

"We'll find him and straighten him out," said Eric. "You need not stay up unless you like."

"Yes, I must," said Julie. "Anyway, there's still the Empire broadcast."

6

Eric went out after the others and took a turn through the streets of the town, up one and down another. He passed the small chapel from which a soft light was filtering through a stained-glass window, and a sound made by some solitary singer came patiently and religiously through a partly open door. This made him think of England, and he smiled to consider that he, for all his supposed cultivation and his travels, was no more free from particular and provincial ties than any other man. A soft, colored light and the music from a hymnbook took him back thousands of miles and dozens of years.

He passed a couple of native boys in white jumpers which turned them into queer apparitions in the darkness and two white men walking slowly together, heads bent as they conversed. But except for these the streets were empty. Up one street and down another Eric went, and the search seemed hopeless. He made his way back to the hotel.

Victor Tolley and George Parrish were in the public bar, drinking beer and conversing importantly in low tones. Victor's face was lighted up, and there was almost a benign look upon it. That was what excitement did to his habitually indolent features.

"Here you are!" Victor said to Eric. "No luck, I presume. Well, that's our story too. I thought I had a glimpse of him, but whoever it was went around a corner, and I lost him. At that I began thinking and made up my mind if it had been him he wouldn't have come back with me. I should have lost him, you see. There's no use to hunt for him singly, for it will take the three of us to use what force is likely to be required. What we want now is careful reasoning and then careful action, with our forces joined."

"But," said Eric, "are you certain he won't wander back himself? Is it a sure thing that he means to decamp?"

"What does it look like?" rejoined Victor. "His outfit is all in his room. He isn't anywhere about the streets that we know. It's so late now that if he were to walk in this minute he could not get his kit together and answer to his name when it's called over there behind the Queens."

"He wouldn't need his kit tonight."

"Oh yes, he would. It's an inspection of some kind—he told me himself. Very strict they are too. With them it's never anything else but the real thing."

Eric nodded gravely and said, "Well, I think you're right. He seems to have levanted."

"My idea is," Victor said, "that he is legging it up the river road. He would have to be on this side, because the ferry doesn't run at night. If I'm right we can overtake him, and if I'm wrong we can come back and have a look at the beach, in case he's hiding out in hopes the rest of them will leave without him in the morning."

"The river road is most likely," said George Parrish.

"Very well, then, we'll be off. This is how we'll handle it. There's nothing to bring a man back quietly and peaceably like a good, heavy blanket such as I have here. The blanket goes over his head, and there we have him, muffled and wrapped, and the matter is as gentlemanly as any application of force can be. Nobody gets hurt, and when we have him brought back here we can show him the light of reason."

"Yes, or unreason," said George Parrish.

Victor took the blanket, which was folded into compact form, and they set out. As they passed the door of the lounge they saw Julie sitting there in front of the wireless. They rounded the corner of the hotel and headed toward the river, past the few houses which stood in that direction.

"Ever take part in a man hunt before?" Eric asked George Parrish.

"Can't say I ever did. Did you?"

"In the war. Not much like this though."

"Did you get your man?"

"There wasn't much left of him, poor chap."

"We must get this one without a scratch," said Victor. "We must take him like a blooming butterfly."

The air was so quiet that they could hear the flow of the river. Overhead the luminous sky was bright with stars, for the night was as large and expansive above as it was small and secretive below. The three searchers were beyond the street lights, and every tree, every bush, every small building was a center of black shadow and mystery.

"Is that someone on the jetty?" asked George Parrish in a whisper.

But it was not. It was some stick of timber lying across a small truck.

"He would have got much farther than this," said Victor.

"He would if he made straight off. He may have lost some time."

"That's true enough," Victor replied. "Nicky went after him at the start, and she may have tried to change him over."

Eric was thinking, "Civilization unfits one for a job like this. The fact that this is an errand of mercy does not alter the fact that it is one of force, and the civilized mind hates force. So do the civilized emotions. I'm as squeamish inside as a small boy out poaching or as a soldier on a night raid. I've got the bad habit of reflection—too much used to looking on instead of doing."

Victor was not thinking. He was all action. At a minimum of inconvenience to himself, he was meeting a crisis. He was rising to an emergency. He had always dreamed that this was the sort of man he really was.

"Look!" Victor said suddenly.

But before he had uttered this word the others had seen

what he had seen, a solitary figure in the middle of the road, clear of the darker shadows.

"We've got him!" said George Parrish. "See his uniform!"

They all saw the glow of starlight where it struck the gold-threaded insignia on the dark blue sleeve. Without a word they advanced, and when their quarry heard their steps and turned they ran upon him. Victor had flung out the blanket, and he threw it with such force that the German was thrown to the ground and flattened, with both Victor and the blanket on top of him. He yelled, but the sound was dampened. Victor tried to make a good job of his blanketing, and then they raised their captive and tied him about the middle with a piece of stout rope which Victor had provided as a lashing to accompany the blanket.

"He struggles hard. Well, that shows he's a game one," Victor said, panting.

"We'd best still his noise a bit more," said Eric, and tied his necktie around the blanket in such a manner that it served as a kind of gag.

"Now walk him, and the quicker the better!" Victor said.

They walked him, hustling him as rapidly as they could over the route back to the Beach Court.

"If we meet anyone, he's drunk," said George Parrish.

"Of course!" said Victor.

But they met no one, although once they paused and waited until a lone pedestrian had gone from the block ahead. The final sprint was the hardest as they ran with their captive, who was only partly self-propelled, and at the last almost hurled him through the hotel door into the office.

"There!" said Eric. "What we've been through for you, my fine young idiot!"

"Stop your thrashing about. I'm only trying to take this hood off you," Victor said.

"He kicked my shin," said George Parrish, dancing about but still trying to lend a hand at restraining the young Nazi.

"Make you think of your school days," said Eric.

"I'd prefer to be reminded in some other way," said George Parrish.

"There it comes!" said Victor. "What an unveiling!"

His laugh was cut short abruptly, and Eric exclaimed, "Good lord, it isn't he!"

The German they had caught was not Hugo Becker, but his one-time companion, Kurt Schaefer, who had elected to stay with the coach drivers instead of at the Beach Court. The one thing which mattered at the moment was that he was not Hugo, and this was all they knew.

Free and blinking in the light, Kurt Schaefer paused only an instant before he set upon them valiantly, evidently under the impression that it was necessary for him to subdue them and to win through to his own kind. He took Victor first, driving him back against the desk and sending the hotel register and inkwell against the farther wall like shrapnel.

"It's only a mistake!" Victor managed to yell, but after that the breath was knocked out of him, and he could not say anything.

Eric and George Parrish tried to seize the German and to explain at the same time, but he ducked and tore and struck at them. George Parrish went down with a bloody cheek but was up again, hanging to Kurt Schaefer's arm and trying to drag him away from Eric, who was putting up a boxer's defense in the old school tradition. All three went milling around the office, crashing into chairs and doors. The fight came to its first pause when Eric and George managed together to fling Kurt back into the center of the room. He could not keep his balance, went down, sprang up again, panting, looking for a new advantage of attack. He saw Julie coming down the stairs, and the presence of a young woman, not without beauty, looking distressed but not alarmed, seemed to mean something to him.

"We got the wrong one," Victor said, rallying once again. "They all look alike. Peas in a pod, they are."

"Hold on!" Eric said to the German. "This can all be explained. We had no designs against you. We took you for someone else."

"Not for a friend evidently," said Kurt grimly, between pants.

"But where is the other one—the right one?" asked Julie.

"We don't know," said Eric. "We thought we had him."

"Look sharp," Victor said. "He's going to give it to you again!"

Eric and George took postures of defense, but Kurt said,

"I am not threatening you. I only tell you not to put your hands on me again."

"Explain to him," said Julie. "This situation is impossible."

"I agree with you," Eric replied, "but the explanation is rather difficult, don't you think?"

"I am waiting for your explanation," said Kurt.

"Well——" Victor began, but he did not get any further, for three German officers walked through the front door.

They looked about them with sharp, hard eyes. George Parrish was bleeding freely about the face, and they were all bloody and soiled, and their clothing was torn. The office, a bare place to begin with, was now deprived of its few comforts and adornments. The only chairs were smashed and thrown about, and the desk was swept clean. The blanket and rope lashing lay on the floor, adding a particularly sinister touch to the scene of combat. Besides looking bloody and soiled, Eric, Victor, and George looked guilty and felt guilty.

The principal officer, who was a tall man with a small mustache and sun-bleached eyebrows, spoke gruffly in German at some length, and Kurt Schaefer, standing at attention, answered him.

"This is an outrage," the officer said in English. "I demand to know the meaning of this violent and unjustifiable attack upon one of our officers and this kidnaping!"

It was Julie who spoke.

"I am afraid, sir, that the explanation can be made to better purpose in the morning," she said.

"Yes," said Eric, recovering his equilibrium, "you shall have our apologies and our explanation, and we will make every effort to satisfy you. This affair is really not at all what it seems."

"Huh!" grunted the officer, and turned to Kurt again, launching another flow of German, to which Kurt replied.

"You have said you mistook this man for someone else. For whom did you mistake him?"

"That's not easy to explain either," said Victor.

"Am I to understand that you do not know who it was you mistook him for?"

Victor shrugged and said nothing.

"I beg of you," said Julie, "let this matter go until morning!"

The officer looked at her gravely but said nothing. The two who were with him said not a word but stood at attention and went on staring.

"This is a strange situation, a remarkable situation!" the officer said. "I do not like it. I do not like it that no one will tell me what this is about. There must be a reason for this blood, this dirt, this disgraceful conduct. . . ."

He spoke again to Kurt Schaefer, and this time Victor and the others could hear him mention the name Becker several times. The German guttural sounded menacing. Schaefer, replying, also pronounced Becker's name more than once.

"Perhaps," the officer began in English, with irony, "I may be permitted to ask as to the whereabouts of Hugo Becker?"

"We don't know where he is," replied Victor.

"He is not here?"

"No, he is not here."

The officer stared at Victor without turning his head or changing his expression, which was one of accusation and distrust. He uttered some short commands, and the two who had come with him went tramping up the stairs. They could be heard walking about on the second floor, in the hall, in the rooms, then going out on the balcony. After a while they came down again and reported in words which evidently put the worst construction upon the facts.

"Oh well," said Victor, "you'll be onto it presently, in any case. You may as well know your chap has turned against Hitler and given you leg bail."

The storm that followed was almost beyond belief, the bellowing, the shouting back and forth in German, the rapid fire of questions, the inability to understand replies. To make things clearer Victor put in some ideas of his own about Hitler, although, as he always said, he was not a man for politics and believed in live and let live. It was the story of this scene and the fury of the German officer which, when communicated to Hugo Becker later, more than anything else disturbed him in his efforts to make normal use of his reason. .

7

Wʜᴇɴ ʜᴜɢᴏ ᴀɴᴅ ɴɪᴄᴋʏ left the hotel they walked a little while, almost at random. Her arm was holding his, and if it had not been she could hardly have kept up, for he strode ahead rapidly, completely absorbed.

"Yes," he said aloud, although he was not talking to her particularly, "I conducted myself badly. It was not nice to reproach her for being what she is. I suppose I should have said, 'Madam, you do not understand what our Führer has done for his people. I will explain to you about the *führer-prinzip.*' Do you think she would have listened to me? Oh no. She would not. They think what they like, that kind."

He lapsed into German, a torrent of words, and Nicky dropped his arm. He had gone several yards before he realized that she was not with him, and then he turned in surprise.

"Nicky, where are you?" he asked, and his voice was not without irritation.

"I don't think it makes any difference to you where I am. I've been dragged quite far enough, after all!"

"Oh, I beg your pardon. I have been so rude. I was walking very fast."

"You should be walking very fast in the other direction, Herr Becker. You forget that your time has run out."

"Yes, yes. I did forget. I do not like that such things should be said. How shameful it was! I have been very angry."

"It's all over now," said Nicky.

"Of course it is. I shall be going away in the morning and I shall never see that woman again."

They were retracing their steps slowly.

"It's been nice knowing you," said Nicky.

"Oh, but I shall not see you again. What an idiot I have been! This is not a proper parting with a new friend. Now I know you are angry with me."

"Why should I be angry with you? I never knew you until today, and tomorrow you will be gone. What a silly waste of emotion!"

They came to the opening of the path which led through to the shore. The path itself they could not see in the darkness, but there was no mistaking the place marked by a break in the fringe of trees along the road.

"Let us walk on the beach, Nicky. It will not require much time. They may send for me if they like, and I will not care. I will make the best excuses I can."

"No," said Nicky. "It is better this way. I wonder how differently things would have had to be in the world for me to have known you and for you to have known me. If I had been born in Düsseldorf I might have been just one of those girls with pigtails. Yet God could have managed it if He had liked. I wanted to meet someone from far off. Well, now I have."

"You are still angry."

"No, I am not. I did not like it when you forgot all about me, as if you did not know that people think bitter things and say bitter things all the time. I could understand the way you acted at first, but to carry on as you did, stamping and raging, marching off in a great fury, dragging me with you!"

"We will have one more look at the sea together, you and I," said Hugo.

"No," said Nicky again. "That is not like you. You do not forget such a thing as duty. I will walk with you as I was going to do, and before you quite reach the place where all the rest of your men are I will disappear in the darkness. You came from far away and you belong far away."

She was taken completely by surprise as he lifted her in his arms, but she offered no resistance, nor did she cry out. She did not know that he was so strong, for he looked slender and light, but he held her and carried her without effort. But the path to the beach was narrow and dark, and he was not sure of his footing. She put one arm about his neck and leaned against him to avoid the branches. Once she had to duck, and her cheek was close against his. He did not put her down until they had emerged upon the white sand and saw the breakers in their moving ranks offshore.

"One little walk together by the sea," said Hugo. "If we had not come here I should always regret my stupidity. Is it forgotten that I was angry?"

"Yes," Nicky said. "I never was really cross with you. I had no right to be. You acted naturally."

"Not the way I want to act," said Hugo. "What color is your hair, Nicky? I cannot tell in the light of the stars."

"You saw it today when the sun was shining."

"Yes, but I did not know the color. I tried to decide, but I could not, because it seemed to change."

"It isn't red."

"No."

"It isn't yellow."

"No."

"It isn't black."

"No. I know all the colors it isn't. I am trying to find out what it is."

"Do you ever laugh, Hugo?"

"Yes, of course I laugh, very often."

"I don't think I have heard you laugh a single time. You have smiled, but when you smile there is something sad about it, as if you were holding back, as if you were not quite sure. Are all young Germans as serious as you?"

"Let me be serious tonight anyway. I laugh out loud when I am gay at home or with friends who are laughing also, but I cannot laugh and think at the same time. If I cannot think I cannot feel—or, at any rate, understand what I am feeling. But tell me, is that what I mean, or am I talking foolishly?"

"That is what you mean, but how can I know whether it is foolish or not?"

"I do not know the color of your hair, but I know how it feels and how it smells. Such a nice fragrance."

"You have never felt my hair."

"It was against my face just now, on the path. I did not like to put you down. I was hoping we would not come to the beach for a long time."

"But it was a long time. It seemed interminable to me!"

"Nicky, you're joking!"

"Yes, but fancy your knowing that I was joking."

Hugo laughed, and when he realized that he was laughing he laughed more loudly.

Nicky was laughing, too, but she said, "We are being exceedingly silly."

They sat down beside one another in the sand and looked at the sky and the pattern of bright stars. Hugo put his arm around her and kissed her on the cheek, on the hair, and on the lips. She found herself holding to him tightly.

"It must be all right for us to be together here," said Nicky softly. "Everything has been against it since we were born, and it couldn't have happened now without some kind of special intervention."

"What an interesting word!" said Hugo.

She giggled, and they were close together for a long time, and neither spoke, because there was nothing they could say which was so important as what they felt, and words could not have matched in delicacy or swiftness, in poignancy or variety the experience of all their senses. They lost awareness of time and of any other reality except their own present companionship under the stars, against the world.

Yet the moment did come when they started up, and whether it was some sound they had heard or some inner reminder that to stay longer was impossible neither of them knew.

"We must go!" said Hugo.

"Yes."

"My poor Nicky!"

"My poor Hugo!"

"But we will not speak of tomorrow."

Silently Nicky emptied the sand from her shoes, and Hugo kneeled to retie the laces. They rose together, looked about them as if to impress upon their memories one last time the aspect and quality of this one night, and then found the path and walked slowly back to the road and to the hotel.

"I will wait until you have gone in," Hugo said.

He stood outside, under the balcony, while Nicky tiptoed through the office and slipped up the stairs. She went so swiftly and with so earnest an intention of being unobserved that she did not notice the havoc through which she passed. The office was only dimly lighted, and quiet had settled over its ruin and its unscrubbed stains of blood.

Hugo lighted a cigarette, puffed at it silently for a few moments, then tossed it away and himself entered the hotel.

He was now wondering what he would say to account for his tardiness, and in back of that he was sad because he had parted from Nicky. All of him was sad. He started to walk slowly and indifferently toward the stairs and almost at once hit against the back of an unsteady chair which promptly collapsed into its component parts, the rungs rattling and rolling on the floor. This seemed to him remarkable, and he stood studying the smashed wood and cane in perplexity.

A door opened, and a voice said, "Who is it?"

Victor Tolley, in an untidy wrapper which only partly concealed his rumpled pajamas, was staring and blinking, and his look was frightened.

"You!" he said, almost in a whisper. "You!"

"Yes," said Hugo, "and why not?"

"You mustn't be seen. They're out after you. You'll be shot, I tell you. I never saw such a commotion about anything."

"I do not understand."

"Come with me. Come into the private bar here. I tell you if you're seen it's all up with you."

Victor hustled Hugo into the bar and shut the door and bade him wait until Eric could be summoned, because two heads were better than one at such a time. Eric came hastily, a silk robe about him, a combination of singular alertness and calm. The shutters of the bar were closed so that no light showed through to be seen from the outside.

"What's to be done?" asked Victor.

"Why should anything be done?" Hugo asked in return.

"I cannot be detained here. I am in a great hurry to report myself."

"Listen to him!" said Victor. "He's stark mad. I tell you they know everything. They're out after you."

"What is it they know? And who are 'they'?"

"The Germans know how you turned against Hitler and did a bolt."

"It's a lie!" cried Hugo in great agitation. Then he asked, "What is it to do a bolt?"

"How you cut and run——"

"I did not run. None of it is true. No! I must see my commanding officer—now—at once!"

He opened the door, but Eric asked sharply, "Where have you been, then, if you didn't mean to give them the slip?"

"Where have I been?"

"Yes," said Victor, "that's it, you see. You'd best give a good account of that if you value your skin."

Hugo felt himself flushing. He was in haste to get away from these men, but he could not help thinking of the white beach, the stars, and Nicky. He did not want to tell where he had been. He was willing to tell anything else, but not that, for was there not in him the spirit of the Teutonic knights of an age of high honor? Could he speak of Nicky, allow himself to be questioned concerning her and why and how they had gone to the beach, suffer her name to be bandied from tongue to tongue grossly?

"I have no time for this foolishness," Hugo said, and

started headlong out of the bar, and then out of the hotel, without pausing to go to his room for his equipment.

Evidently something of serious import had taken place—he could not imagine what. The uncertainty was terrifying, for from the first moment he did not question the reality, the full-bodied reality of the predicament which Victor and Eric had sought to urge upon him. This predicament was still vague of substance, but it was real, for elements suggested to the imagination are apt to strike most quickly and deeply into the literal mind. Hugo's mind was trained to obedience and method, but he had imagination as well as this blunt literalness, so that he was doubly at a disadvantage. His sense of guilt at having overstayed his permitted time, small in reason but much larger in emotional effect, was quickly swollen to sinister proportions. He was burdened with it.

He started to cross the square toward the Queens Hotel, but he had gone only a little way when he felt that he was being followed, not openly but with stealth. He did not doubt that either Victor or Eric had come after him, and he resented this stalking hotly. It added also to his anxiety, and he needed to take the situation into his own hands. He slowed his steps and was ready to wheel about quickly, fists doubled, but before he could do so he was seized roughly from behind. He flung himself around and at the same moment struck as hard as he could, so that his assailant was half thrown, half knocked to the ground.

Hugo looked down. To his amazement he discovered that he had laid out one of his own kind, a boy named

Werner, whom he knew well. Werner had struck the ground with considerable force, his head hitting against a root of the big tree, and he did not stir at once.

"He was choking me as if I had been a villain," Hugo said to himself, and now his sense of guilt was stronger than anything else, and the reality of this predicament—the nature of which he still could not comprehend—was thrice greater than before.

In reason, there were two choices—to go forward or to go back—but his excited instinct recognized only one, and he retreated to the hotel as quickly as he could. He was drawing away from forcible capture, from immediate physical danger, and in so doing he was magnifying the larger problem. Victor and Eric were in the hotel office, and they hustled him through to the private bar again—but not before he had seen, this time, the stains of blood upon the floor. Hugo looked into Eric's face and then into Victor's. No, they did not believe in his innocence—they would not. It was hopeless. But why? He had intended no wrong. What could have happened?

"The situation is simply this," Eric said slowly. "Your commanding officer is under the impression that you were led to repudiate the things which Hitler stands for and to run off. I may say that we have been under the same impression, and for that reason we have been and are ready to help you. After all, old fellow, this is hardly the time to change your mind again."

"But I have not changed my mind. I cannot understand——"

"That kind of thing can't be explained away," Victor said. "You'll never think of a story half good enough, not if you puzzle all night. We've been running risks to help you and are in a bit of trouble on account of it, but we don't mind that. The thing for you to do is to hop it quick and get clean away. Then you can puzzle as much as you like and decide what's to be done next."

"What he says is true, old fellow," said Eric, nodding in a kindly way. "Your position here is insupportable."

Hugo said to himself, his lips moving soundlessly, "I will not tell where I have been," for it was in his mind that to mention Nicky now would be to throw her into a major scandal. Yet all this nonsense about turning against Hitler was still a puzzle.

"Well," said Victor, "what is it to be? I tell you what I'll do. I'll send my best native boy with you as a guide. There is nothing he doesn't know about trails and tracking and the lay of the land everywhere hereabouts. He can hide you where nobody will find you and shoot springbok for you to eat. With Jacob to look after you, there's no doubt about your getting clear. He could stir up the natives to fight for you, if needed, but I wouldn't let him go as far as that if I were in your shoes."

"Good!" said Eric. "That's the ticket. You must hide out until your ship has sailed and they have stopped looking for you. Now there's no time to be lost. Call your boy Jacob at once, Tolley, and you, Becker, scuttle up to your room and make a pack of the things you need. Only bare essentials, you understand."

At the moment Hugo did not realize the irrevocable nature of flight. It began to seem to him a temporary solution, for he knew that he was somehow turned into a quarry for his own people. He could not go to them, not after feeling Werner's strength against him, not after striking Werner down—not with Nicky as a current running through his mind. As for all the rest, he could not fathom it now, but with a little time he might clear it up. Innocence was not safeguard enough upon occasions of fury (but indeed he did not feel innocent); one needed knowledge; one had to be informed.

Yet Hugo did not really make a choice. He was rushed into doing what he did by Victor and Eric, who thought it was for the best, and their urging influenced him more then he knew. Almost blindly, his head whirling, he mounted the stairs. At the top he met Nicky, and tears were coming from her eyes, down her cheeks.

"Oh, Hugo," she said, "I know! Julie has told me. How can such a cruel, stupid thing have happened? I do not understand—I will never understand! It is not right. No, it is not! It is not fair. But you must go, now, before you are caught. You will never be able to disprove what has been told against you."

He took her in his arms and held her.

"Almost the worst thing for me," Nicky said, "is that I do not know you. I realize that now. All the little things I should have asked you while there was still time—all the things one has a right to know——"

"What do you want to ask me, Nicky?"

"When is your birthday, Hugo?" She laughed hysterically. "That's silly, isn't it? But I want to know about you, Hugo, all the things a girl in Düsseldorf would know. It's important, but I'm too late."

"My birthday is the first of November," Hugo told her, hugging her tight. "I like the smell of grapes which grow in my country and butter without salt and girls with hair which is not red nor black, nor yet brown nor yellow, but something of both and in between."

"Tell me more!" Nicky pleaded, pressing her lips against his cheek.

"If there could only be more time, another day, another hour! Nicky, listen to me carefully. My parents are going to be at Durban. I was hoping to meet them there, but that will not be possible now. They are coming in the *Pretoria* on her next voyage, the end of the month, and you can find out from the newspaper when she is arriving. Will you go to Durban and see them and tell them what you can about me that may make them feel happier? Will you do this?"

"Yes," said Nicky, sobbing, "and I will get them to tell me about you."

Eric was coming up the stairs, full of crisp impatience.

"There is no time to be lost," they heard him say. "Someone was just tramping past the door, and there's something going on in the square. They are still hunting. Can I help you throw your things together?"

Nicky stepped into the shadows and dried her eyes. She watched them go into Hugo's room and stood in the doorway and looked on as they spread out a blanket and began collecting the articles Hugo was to take upon his flight. Suddenly Hugo was about to straighten up from where he was kneeling at a bureau drawer and tell them that this was all nonsense, that he was not going away. But there was a pain in his right hand, with which he had struck Werner, and he thought of that encounter with dread. Why had he been seized so earnestly?

"Not ready yet?" called Victor from the bottom of the stairs, not loudly, but clearly enough to be heard.

"Coming!" Eric answered.

Julie had appeared from her room, and she stood beside Nicky, silently, not saying a word. Her face was still and cold, but the light pouring through the doorway glinted in her eyes, and they seemed to glow.

Hugo's bundle was completed in a few moments more and fastened with a belt. He thrust into his pocket an automatic pistol which was not part of his outfit but issued on the *Schleswig-Holstein* for small-arms exercises.

"There," said Eric, "you've got what you need, but you'll be traveling light. That's as it should be."

Down the stairs they went, Hugo first, Eric following, then Nicky, then Julie like an apparition.

"Good!" said Victor when he saw them. "Jacob is out here at the back. You can trust him. I've told him what he is to do for you. He has a good lot of food and water and a kitchen knife to skin carcasses and so on, the best thing I could find. Too bad there's no biltong about the place. By rights you should have biltong for a trek such as you're taking on."

They went through the bar to a door which opened upon an enclosure at the rear, and when it was open they saw Jacob standing there, smiling. Even in the darkness his smile was visible because of his white teeth. He was wearing the same greatcoat with dangling braid in which he wrapped himself habitually.

"He will wear that coat," Victor said. "If he don't go fast enough make him throw it off. Here, you take this hat of mine. It won't give you away so easy as yours."

Hugo put on the hat which Victor handed him, a sprawly brown felt with holes punched in it.

"You're off!" said Eric. "Good luck!"

He shook Hugo's hand, and Victor shook it also and uttered a hearty "Good luck!" on his own account. Hugo looked for Nicky, but she was not to be seen. She had run ahead in the darkness and intercepted him at the corner of the yard.

"I wanted to give you something to take, Hugo," she said, "but there's only this." She kissed him.

"You're not crying?"

"Not any more."

"That's right. We will not always be parted."

"No," she said, but she felt that this was not true.

She felt that it was not true, but, just the same, she smiled, and he smiled, until in the darkness they could not see any longer. Hugo and Jacob were heading for the river, keeping close to the houses, ready to dodge out of sight if a hostile step should sound. They went stealthily themselves, but Nicky could hear them. By holding her breath it seemed to her that she could hear them almost until they reached the river road.

There was no use waiting any longer, and she was tired. Her weariness was suddenly so great that it could hardly be borne, yet as she went back into the hotel she peered into Victor's face.

"I don't see why he had to go away," she said. "I can't think what it was you told about him and why you told it and how you happened to have a fight with that other German. . . . In fact, Victor, I am suspicious of you. . . ."

She was so tired that she sounded mournful rather than angry. Besides, what was done was done. She knew that.

"Don't fret, Nicky," said Victor. "We pulled him out of it, didn't we? It would have been a bad night for that chap if we hadn't. He went off his nut in a way, I suppose. At least, that's how I account for it. Perhaps it's just as well he's out of Mr. Hitler's navy, because he would be bound to run up against it sometime, the sort he is.

"You look droopy, Nicky. Won't you have a drink? You were out looking for him, too, weren't you? You should have left all that to us. No wonder you're tired, come to think of it, after a go like that. Well, I rather think I will have a drink. I need one."

As he watched the beer flow Victor added reflectively, "You never did have any opinion of me when it came to action, did you, Nicky? Well, I wonder if you won't change your mind after tonight!"

8

Nicky had not slept. In the morning she got out of bed, slipped on a wrap, and stood on the balcony, as if there must be something she had been waiting in agony all night long to see. The light was flat and gray, and the square was damp. At first she thought it was deserted, but then she noticed one of the Germans in uniform, standing motionless against the ancient cannon under the big tree. It was as if he was manning the rusty artillery piece against some assault to come. He was looking across and up at her, and she could see his face, but there was no expression in it.

She went back to her room and dressed hastily. As she tried to fix her hair she noticed that her hands were shaking. She held them out before her and watched them tremble. She told herself that it was no good, that she had to be calm.

She hurried downstairs as quietly as possible, but there was no need for stealth because Victor, Eric, and Julie were standing in the lounge, talking, intent on their own words, at the expense of noticing anything else. Nicky stood listening for a minute or two.

"I knew the hotel was being watched," Victor said. "I could feel it all night, you know. Wherever you look there's one of those sober-looking chaps—enough to take away your appetite."

"I don't understand it," Julie said.

"I shouldn't wonder if they expect to find their man concealed somewhere about and think it's unlikely he would have made for the interior," Eric remarked. "Well, if that's it, the beggars are wrong this time."

Victor sounded uneasy, although he was putting on a show of great confidence. He said, "There's no use getting the wind up. Common assault and battery's all they can get us for, as I look at it. They can't prove anything else, much as they may try, because they've no witnesses. I can't say I want to be jugged, but if it comes to that we'll just have to stick it."

"I shall be surprised if there's any action through your police at all," Eric said thoughtfully. "It wouldn't give them the kind of satisfaction they're interested in, and the evidence certainly would not make good reading, especially if it got into the papers overseas."

"It would be a black eye," Victor declared.

"Yes, it would. They don't want their propaganda off-set or diluted, do they? What they're really interested in, no doubt, is getting young Becker back again. I daresay he's got them mystified, and that must make matters a great deal worse. They don't know what he'll do, you see, and with all he knows about the inside of their game he might be embarrassing to have on the loose."

"Who will they notify? How will they manage?" asked Julie in her aloof voice which had, nevertheless, a curious inflection of great interest.

"They have their own ways of handling such matters, you may be sure," Eric said.

"That they have," Victor was quick to agree. "Underground ways . . . devious ones."

Nicky did not wait to hear any more. She crossed the office quickly, went through the front door, and circled the outside of the hotel to the kitchen, where she got herself some coffee. She drank two cups, and the sensation of the blood returning to her cheeks reminded her that it had been gone for a long time. She had been so cold and rigid that it seemed incredible she could have been moving about without breaking into pieces. Now she felt that she could keep from shaking like a dummy on springs, and she left the Beach Court and walked toward the Queens. She was so certain of what she was going to do, so prepared for every step, that it was as if she had been through it all before, instead of merely having rehearsed it during the unspeakable night. She seemed to be remembering instead of anticipating.

Groups of Germans in uniform stood in front of the Queens, and they had to part to let her pass through. As they did so they looked at her intently, without smiling. Inside the hotel door she paused, looking for the one to whom to make her request. She chose the nearest German boy.

"I should like to see your commanding officer."

He appeared to be surprised and unfriendly.

"Please. I must see him."

"Who shall I announce, and on what business?" asked the boy in the same stiff, precise English she had heard from Hugo.

She gave her name and added, "It is about this—this affair last night."

The boy's face had become a mask. He disappeared, and she was left standing alone, aware of the close scrutiny she was undergoing. But she remained calm, glad that she had come this far and that there was no going back. The waiting, the inability to be doing something was the hard thing. Yet she found that she was by no means through with the hard thing, not by several hours and hundreds of seconds, slow-passing and silent, for the German boy had returned to say the commandant was not in and that she was to wait. He conducted her to a room just off the lower hall and asked her to be seated.

"How long before I can see him? It's important."

"I cannot say."

She sat down, and he left her alone. In spite of herself she began noticing things in which she was not interested, things which were trivial and tedious. The bed was made up, and it occurred to her that maid service at the Queens

must be a great deal more efficient than it was in the Beach
Court, where rooms often were not put to rights until almost noon. Then she realized what must have been the real
truth, that the bed had not been slept in the night before.
There were some toilet articles on the bureau, together with
a leather belt and a few papers. On the other chair a blue
coat was lying. She noticed that the mosquito-net canopy
over the bed did not seem to have a single patch or hole.
After a little while she was tired of looking at such things
and of having to think about them, and she moved her chair
to the window.

She could look out toward the Beach Court, unfamiliar
when viewed at such an angle. A German was still stationed
near the old cannon, but whether he was the same one she
had seen earlier she could not tell. The sky was overcast,
and the square was still damp and dull. This long delay had
been no part of her calculation, and she found it hard to
restrain her impatience.

"Will he never come?" she asked out loud, but there was
no reply.

It was almost ten o'clock before she happened to see,
with startled eyes, the German commandant emerging from
the front door of the Beach Court and then crossing the
square, with two uniformed figures beside him.

Eric had acted as the principal spokesman. He had said
that they all regretted the unpleasant incident exceedingly
and that they were sorry they could offer no amends for

the violence unintentionally committed except their apologies—and, of course, their readiness to be responsible if charges were brought. He said they were sorry they could give no information whatever as to the present whereabouts of Hugo Becker.

"You mean you can give no information or that you will give none?" inquired the German officer.

"I think it is fair to say that we can give none," said Eric.

"I am afraid I must differ with you, Herr Williams. I was not, as you say, born yesterday. It is too much for me to believe that you cannot suggest some interesting possibilities as to Becker and the arrangements he must have made."

Eric shrugged. Julie looked at the commandant with cool hostility, but so far he had paid no attention to her whatever.

"Come, come! We are wasting time. I have a right to demand that you confide in me what you know." The officer looked from one to another of the three, even at Julie now, and suddenly he snapped out the question, "Is he here? Have you hidden him?"

Victor started to speak, but Eric cut in smoothly, "We have not seen Becker. We do not know where he is."

"I warn you, sir, this is a grave affair."

"We are answerable to the laws of this country," said Eric. "You are at liberty to bring charges."

"There will be no charges of the kind you mean. You will please not take me for a fool. I am not interested in child's play. Now, Mr. Proprietor, you will not object if my men search your premises? I am confident that you do not desire to give protection to a deserter."

"Come ahead and search," said Victor. "I will show your chaps all about the place."

The officer gave his orders in German, and they all felt that the search would be thorough.

"I am thinking that we shall find Becker yet," said the commandant to Eric. "He would not have been fool enough to go away on foot. It would be so easy to catch him. I know that he did not leave by car, horse, or plane. So you see"—and here he smiled slowly and grimly—"I am thinking he will turn up."

But he did not turn up. In half an hour Victor returned with the Germans who had made the search, and they reported at length. The commandant questioned them sharply. Then he turned to Eric, Victor, and Julie and had them go over the whole story again, testing it, turning it, watching for some slip, some implausible expression which he might have missed before. The thing which puzzled them most was his insistence that not one but two of his men had been assaulted the previous night. They could not make this out, and evidently he did not understand or believe their protestations of ignorance.

At last he decided to let the matter rest and, without a further word, with no more than an abrupt movement of his head, turned away and left them, accompanied by his aides.

"Well," said Eric, "that's that!"

"It was your leer that put him in such a temper," Julie said to Victor.

"I never leer," said Victor.

"I wish you could see yourself. From the instant he said there would be no charges you began looking like a cat with a canary safe inside."

The three Germans walked diagonally across the square, the commandant a little ahead of the others, to reach the Queens Hotel in the shortest way. As soon as they arrived the commandant must have been told about Nicky's presence, for he appeared in the doorway of the room where she was waiting. He looked at her for a minute or two and then evidently decided to talk with her alone.

"You wish to see me?"

"Yes," said Nicky, and she waited while he took up a position immediately in front of her, standing erect but with his feet a little apart. She went on, "You may as well let me tell you in my own way. I want to help Hugo Becker."

"That is very kind of you."

"No, it isn't kind. That's what I want you to know— he's not in need of kindness, because he didn't do anything— he didn't say anything, really. I know that, and if you only can see the truth you will not hold anything against him. Oh, I know that some strange things happened, and I can't explain all of them—I don't even want to try . . . they don't matter, you see, they don't matter at all.

"I saw Hugo last night. I talked with him, and he was proud and happy, and he had everything to live for. He was a loyal German and still is, and you must not believe anything else. I am telling you what I know. You do believe me, don't you?"

The commandant did not answer at once. He stood looking at her, frowning slightly, his sun-bleached eyebrows drawn together.

"Why did he run away?" he asked suddenly.

"I don't know. He didn't want to. He was late in reporting because of a little scene for which he was not responsible and because he was walking with me. Then you were hunting him, and they told him something dreadful had happened and that he was mixed up in it in some terrible way, and they made him believe his only chance was to escape. I can't tell you anything about that part of it, because I haven't it straight myself, but I do know he was really loyal and is now. His life mustn't be ruined, and it will be unless you are willing to believe in him. Surely he deserves to be trusted in spite of appearances. Why should one terrible half-hour be counted against everything else he ever did?"

The German moistened his lips and stood there in silence, staring at her until she became uneasy.

"Well," Nicky said, "suppose he did say or do some little thing without meaning it? It's what he really is that counts, isn't it?"

"You do not think anyone paid him to run away, do you, Fräulein?" asked the commandant.

"No, of course not."

"You do not think he would be persuaded to do other bad things, just as he was persuaded to run away?"

"No, no. Never."

"Perhaps he did not run away, after all," suggested the commandant. "Perhaps he is just hiding somewhere about, aided by those who do not want him to rejoin his comrades."

"No," said Nicky. "He did go. I know that. I lay awake all night hoping that he would come back, listening for his footsteps."

"Do you know where he went? What did they tell him when he left?"

"I can't say anything more unless you will believe in me and in him," said Nicky. "Can't you see that all I want to do is to help Hugo——?"

The commandant turned brusquely and started out of the room, Nicky hastening to follow. She was at his side when he reached the street, pleading with him, trying to make herself heard, but he paid no attention. He was giving orders in German with a loud, clear voice, rather higher in pitch than his speaking tones.

There was a large maroon automobile standing near the hotel door. It was covered with red mud and dust, and the front part was soiled with rusty water which had overflowed from a capless radiator. Nicky noticed this much as she stood there helplessly and watched the car fill with Germans, heard the motor start and roar. Almost before she could realize what was happening the car was turning into the river road, raising dust behind it in spite of the damp morning. There was nothing she could do.

She said to herself that it had all been useless, that she

had only put Hugo into greater peril; yet she had tried to tell the truth, to appeal to the commandant's sense of fairness and of reality. Perhaps the trouble was that nobody had hold of reality any more. Let some chain of circumstance start, and it whirled people along with it, as in a dream, and they could not see black and white before their eyes, and anyone who could see plain facts was doubted. But she had no great intensity of feeling now, for she was past that, and the reaction had come, a kind of lassitude and numbing. She saw graver danger and graver trouble ahead, but she faced them more calmly than she had faced the lesser, or when she had held more hope. Yet she still hoped, desperately, for Hugo, although every bit of reason so far seemed tumbled and dispersed.

"Where have you been?" Victor asked her when she got back to the Beach Court. "You gave me a scare, Nicky. I've been looking all over for you."

"Well, you don't need to look any more," she said. "I'm here now, and I'm not going away again."

She went upstairs to her room and met Julie in the hallway.

"I'm afraid there's nothing anyone can do," Julie said.

"I know. I've tried, and it's no good."

Julie followed her into her room and sat beside her as she lay down on the bed. Julie stroked her forehead, and it was queer, because she felt as if there were a statue sitting beside her bed, a statue of a strange and distant woman with cool, unrevealing features. But the statue spoke.

"You feel like clutching at straws," Julie said, "but that

won't last. You wouldn't want him back, because he was
not one of their kind——"

"What do you know about it?" Nicky demanded.
"Wasn't he just human like any of us, and didn't he know
where he belonged? Why should he want to ruin his whole
life and be an outcast?"

"You love that German boy, don't you?"

"Yes."

"But there's Victor. He can't see anybody but you. Don't
you care about him?"

"I don't know," said Nicky.

Later that afternoon she thought of one more straw
which might be worth grasping. Hugo was fleeing alone,
except for Jacob, into a strange continent. There must be
people who might be on the watch for him, ready to help
him. But who? She thought of her aunt in Johannesburg,
but she was no good for the purpose; what was needed was
a man, a man of the world, too, with some shrewdness. A
few possibilities suggested themselves, but she was not
satisfied, because the requirements were so special.

Then she remembered Mr. Hickey of the Union Brewery and his assurances of friendship. He traveled constantly
from place to place. He had a quick eye and a resilient
manner. He had seemed knowing, and she recalled that he
had referred once or twice to his powerful connections in
government circles. Yes, Mr. Hickey would do.

She went to the hotel office, found his full name in Victor's disorderly file, and wrote to him a long letter of
appeal. He was, she thought, a rather common sort of

person, but she relied upon his toughness as well as upon his friendly inclinations. She told him that Hugo was innocent of wrongdoing, that he had gone forth with Jacob as his only guide and support and that she hoped Mr. Hickey would be watchful and, if occasion offered, friendly and generous. She marked her letter for the air mail and posted it before she lapsed into despair and exhaustion.

When Victor questioned her again about her preoccupation of that day she told him exactly what she had done. He looked with surprise into her bright, defiant eyes, but he did not say much.

"You'll be lucky if you haven't upset things," he concluded. "I hate to think of it. . . . But don't haggle over it, and don't cry, because what is done is done. . . . What I can't make out is why you should have flustered yourself. Can't you see how calmly I've been taking it? And I was in it worse than anybody, wasn't I? A hostess at a hotel doesn't need to go too far about the guests, I shouldn't think."

9

Hᴜɢᴏ ᴀɴᴅ ᴊᴀᴄᴏʙ climbed a long and twisting road into
the hills, a road that was notched along the edges of deep
valleys and about the round tops of summits which looked
like vast domes in the starlight. Every accent of the countryside was not only strange to Hugo, but, because it was
strange, terrible also. He felt himself lost in a place of torment, a fugitive without any possible sanctuary. His exile
was already all about him, and he was accused, challenged,
awed, and driven with remorse at every step he took. The
realization had come to him suddenly that flight is final and
that one can never flee partway—one must go on and on.

The night was still beautiful, but the hills and valleys,
conventionalized into black masses with unexpected seg-
ments of deep shadow and shafts of reflected light, suggested an element of the grotesque. They partook of cari-

cature, and in Hugo's teeming mind this was more awful than anything else. There was no link between this countryside and himself, no possible tie of understanding. He felt himself menaced, yet there was nothing more disturbing than the native cattle which now and then were awakened and sent lumbering off into the farther darkness.

Jacob walked a few paces ahead, an absurd figure in his trailing black coat which hid every indication of his own natural form and, so far as Hugo was concerned, of his humanity. He was a mock creature, a part of the gigantic caricature, the travesty of which Hugo had unwillingly become a victim. Hugo's eyes kept staring at his back, and he felt himself subordinate to this clumsy shadow, this affront of a low and jesting nature.

At first it was a relief to climb and to be moving, and Hugo threw himself into the exertion as into a measure of immediate protection, but, although he was in excellent physical condition, his muscles soon ached from the unaccustomed movement of climbing. The road sometimes went down, in order to go up again, but it never leveled off. Before long Hugo had to sit down by the roadside to ease the unremitting strain, but no sooner had he paused than he felt a panic to be hastening forward. His anxiety was increased as he was aware of Jacob's eyes fixed upon him, and he sprang to his feet, and they both went on again. Hugo had not addressed a word to Jacob, and the longer the silence continued the more burdensome it became and the more difficult to break, until the muteness fitted in with all the other grotesque elements of the night.

After a few hours, however, the countryside had ceased to trouble Hugo so acutely, and he began to think over the reasons for his flight. When he left Port Quentin he was raised to a high emotional pitch, and the scene with Nicky had played upon his imagination, but now all that seemed suddenly far behind him.

He began to consider on what slight evidence, for what apparently negligible cause he had become a fugitive on a strange continent and sacrificed his career and his citizenship in the fatherland that was dear to him. There was, at last, a lightening in the sky around the horizon, and now it seemed to him incomprehensible that he should have allowed himself to be swayed by the fictitious excitement of Victor and Eric, excitement which he could not now understand—yet, to be sure, it was Eric's calm which had given such contagion to Victor's melodrama. He did not think of either of them as malicious or scheming, not yet, at any rate, but rather looked upon them as a couple of madmen.

Why had he not reported himself at once, in spite of everything, and answered any accusations which might have been leveled at him? In spite of Werner's attack and the violence to which he had resorted himself, why had he not gone on? Certainly he knew his country and his countrymen better than those two Englishmen. He should not have taken their word for anything. On the contrary, he should have doubted them on every point, and all efforts to deter him from his one clear course should have been defied and overridden. This much was plain, but something which was not plain was a troubling, ineradicable impression that somehow his explanations would have done him no good, that he would have been thrown back by an absolute of absolutes. Yet when this impression was strongest he was most certain that he should have faced the consequences, that he should have met death, if necessary, under orders. The idea fitted into something which was old and deep within him.

But at times he began to suspect, with a self-accusation which was torture, that he had really wanted, for some strange reason, to flee. No! No! He denied the possibility. Yet the thought was there, and perhaps that was why his own people would have frowned upon him, judged him, and his explanations and professions proved of no avail. Certainly he had been swept from reason and duty by that girl, Nicky. As to those moments with her at the head of the stairs at the hotel, he had enjoyed them in some exaggerated way. They had wrung his heart, but he had enjoyed them. He had felt himself a hero, a martyr, with the grandeur of renunciation and the nobility of exile.

Was it possible that he had wanted to remain on the same continent with Nicky, that he had become so infatuated with her that he desired to escape from all the forces of honor, duty, and devotion which were to have taken him away from her and into a career which would have kept them forever apart? If so, this was a weakness to be condemned bitterly.

He began to blame her for what he was suffering on her account. He had protected her good name at the expense of his own, and there was no good reason why he should have done so. He had not been at fault in the first place, and his career was more important than hers.

"Why," he said to himself, "she is not even beautiful. She has a snub nose. I do not know anything about her, who her parents are, where she was born, and what blood flows in her veins."

But he realized that he had felt a dread of exposure on his own account too. He did not want to be questioned and have to relate how he had played fast and loose with his duty and remained, by free choice, with a girl he had known only a day. He was ashamed. It was humiliating to have a ridiculous explanation in a time of great furor. He remembered other times, too, when he had felt impelled to choose some desperate alternative rather than to submit to an airing of his own shame in some relatively trivial matter. He wanted to avoid looking so deeply into his own motives, but he could not. The moving procession of thoughts kept on, and he could not deny that desperation often magnified itself far beyond the occasion which prompted it in the first place. Had this happened in his own case just now?

He could not know the truth of his own conduct, except that he had balanced the German Reich against an affair with a girl and had allowed the Reich to come off second best. And the strange countryside and the absurd figure of the black boy mocked him.

"Why am I running away?" he asked himself. "Why? It was that I was out with a girl and was afraid to say so, because I am supposed to be a gentleman, like one of those knights in the Middle Ages. But no. Those knights would

not have done as I did. The weakness was mine, not theirs.
I was being hunted as a criminal, and I was afraid. When I
felt those hands of that Werner around my neck I was no
longer myself. I hit him, and that was what made me lose
my head and give way to fear. Then I let those two madmen tell me what danger I was in. If I had known they were
mad I might have behaved differently and much better, but
I did not suspect. It is certain that they were mad, however.

"But it was also that I liked to have that girl hang about
my neck and say those things to me. She made me run away
as much as anyone. I was taken in by all that show, by all
of them, fool that I am!"

The oftener he turned these thoughts in his mind, reject-
ing one only to have it succeeded by another more accus-
ing and disquieting, the more convinced he was that he
should not have fled. Even after he had started his flight
he should have turned back. It would not have been too
late. And if the stern countenance of the fatherland had
judged him severely, that was what he should have deserved
and should have undertaken to suffer.

But the remarkable thing about this reasoning was that
the decisive moment was always the one just past. His flight
had not been inevitable two hours ago, or one hour ago,
or ten minutes ago, but now it was. If only he had altered
his foolish decision and gone back—even two minutes ago,
when he was considering the whole situation in this vein—
but now, for some reason which he did not try to define
but was yet perfectly clear and explicit, his course had be-

come irrevocable. Thus he was being committed anew to his folly every moment that passed, although he complained and fought mentally against it.

When daylight had come it seemed to him that they were far up in the hills, but he could not tell, because the land-scape was always the same. The bright grass sparkled in the sun and stretched out, fenceless and almost unbroken, for mile upon mile. But there were countless circles of native huts, wattle and daub, scattered on all sides between him and the horizon, the kraals of the old tribes for which these territories were reserved. Now and then the road passed a thicket or a few tall trees standing together. Soon Hugo saw not only the native huts and the cattle but the natives themselves, trekking or sitting in the sun by the roadside.

He saw madcap girls, naked above the waist, and boys, entirely naked, who called to him, "*Sanka! Sanka!*" and many men wrapped in blankets, and with curious marks on their faces, who stared at him without expression. This scrutiny he did not like, and in spite of himself he was afraid. He did not know that all these natives were taxpay-ers and members of a representative government, and the strangeness of the country was as great by day as by night.

Whenever Hugo looked at Jacob the boy was smiling. Evidently he had no notion of the seriousness of the expedi-tion, or, if he had, he could put an extraordinarily light face upon it. In either case Hugo resented him and the fact that he himself was compelled to rely upon such a guide to find safety.

"It is time to eat, baas," Jacob said.

They were both hungry, and they sat down in the grass beside the road and ate, Jacob sitting a little apart. The food which Victor had put in the pack was good—cold meats, for the most part, and clusters of small and rather greenish bananas which were coarse but satisfying. After they had eaten they went on again, but the sun was high, and they were both weary.

The exertion of walking had become so great that Hugo could hardly bear it, yet he could not bring himself to suggest a halt. Fortunately, they soon came to a group of trees which was near the road, and Jacob said they should sleep. Hugo concealed himself as best he could in the shade, but Jacob lay mostly in the sun, still wrapped in his greatcoat. Almost at once Hugo was asleep, and he slept soundly for a long time. It seemed to him later that he had dreamed of Nicky, but he was not sure whether there had been a real dream or only a recurrence of a longing which now seemed very old and in his wakening quickly vanished.

He started into the urgency of flight again, as if the danger threatening him were only a few seconds past. All the walking they had done, although the road wound and looped, was in the same general direction, away from the sea. But now that they had renewed their march a surprising thing happened. Jacob suddenly decreed a change. They had been overtaking a native boy who walked along with a concertina, trimmed with red tassels, and played as he went. To Hugo's ear it did not seem that the boy made music, but there was a continual outpouring of sound which did, after a while, seem to have some relationship to the afternoon sun, the bare red earth of the road, and the endless spreading of the round hills. This boy with the concertina took a diverging road, to the right, which was apparently the north, and Jacob followed him.

"Why do you turn here?" Hugo asked.

"We follow him, baas," said Jacob.

"Why do we follow him?"

Jacob began to tell a story which concerned a deep jungle and a white princess who lived in a treetop, but Hugo's eyes were hot, his mouth was dry, and he could not keep his attention fixed on the rambling tale. Jacob's words were singsong, and they seemed no more rational than the sounds made by the concertina ahead, though both were related to the road and the endless steps they took. To Hugo all was part of the same mocking.

"Close your mouth!" he said angrily, and Jacob was still.

The new road, which was narrower and not so well traveled as the old, led upward, and for some distance it branched off slowly. Here Hugo looked downward and saw an automobile, evidently a maroon automobile well adorned with mud and dust, steam issuing from its radiator, carrying as passengers a number of figures in uniforms of navy blue. It was odd that these men had not seen Hugo, except that they were hastening in one direction, and he in another. Suddenly, on an impulse, Hugo ran down the slope, yelling as loudly as he could, but by this time the automobile was far off, hidden in dust. He was frightened by the sound of his own voice, by what it meant, and he was glad that the car had gone.

Now it was as if he had been running down that slope to meet death, to die surely, slowly, and completely. He could not explain this feeling, but it was strong and fascinating. Although he was glad that he had not succeeded in attracting the attention of the Germans who were his own friends of yesterday, this thought of the inevitable course of death was not without satisfaction and a moody sense of peace. It was something to contemplate.

Jacob had not indicated any interest in the episode. They walked on, more rapidly, because the boy with the concertina had gained distance. Hour after hour they walked, and once again the sun went down and the stars came out. Still they walked, and at last the concertina player vanished into a native hut near the road, and they were alone again.

They came out on a level place where there were many trees, and it must have been extremely high. Hugo was aching from fatigue, and without a word he collapsed on the ground, which was still warm. After a little he opened his eyes again.

"How far have we traveled, do you think?" he asked Jacob.

Jacob had walked on farther to the edge of the high place, for it ended in a sudden and giddy drop, and peered over the rim. Far below he saw the familiar lights of Port Quentin. He and Hugo were on the heights immediately above the town from which they had fled.

"How far?" asked Hugo again. He was too weary to

raise himself on the ground. "Can anyone overtake us now?"

Jacob chose his words carefully, for he saw a certain likelihood that the baas might be seriously displeased.

"They would have to fly, baas," he said, and gazed down again, with no little curiosity, at the village made so strange and small by the height which separated him from its roofs and its streets. In the starlight the red roofs did not gleam.

10

Aʟʟ ɴɪɢʜᴛ ʟᴏɴɢ Hugo's body twitched and tossed and in its helpless way tried to escape, to return, to grasp the safety of some elusive fancy, to fight off the pursuing realities of the day before. And then it tried to go plodding through the motions to which it had been forced, hour after hour of waking. By some miracle, which was one of the healing processes of nature but no less a miracle on that account, he woke in the morning refreshed and relaxed. His nervous fever had been worn away. His body ached badly, but his exhaustion was past.

He opened his eyes and saw that the sun was shining. The air was gentle.

"Now," he said to himself, "I am a deserter. I am a fugitive. I can never go back. There is nothing for me to live for."

Yet the air was still gentle, and the sun was still shining. He sat up and looked around. Jacob was already awake, sprawled in the grass a short distance away, his hands under the back of his head, peering into the sky. Hugo watched him for a little while.

"What do you see up there?" he asked.

"Only the clouds, baas."

"Do you always smile at the clouds as you are doing now?"

"No, baas. These are good clouds. One time I was high up, higher than the big cloud there. It was very good. I went fast, like the wind."

Hugo fancied that this was some native nonsense, and he had no taste for it. He would have had even less if he had known that Jacob was drawing upon his memories of the Tarzan moving picture and an airplane which had been shown winging into the jungle, but this Hugo had no reason to suspect. Many of the white men of the country were like Hugo, for, although they had taken the land away from Jacob's people, they still assumed that a boy like him would be as completely a master of its secrets as his ancestors. They looked to him for what had used to be—perhaps not the whole substance but at least the general tenor—and never thought that he might be sharing in the present what they had produced for themselves.

It annoyed Hugo that he, a German, and Jacob, a Kaffir, should be conversing with some precision in a language which belonged to neither of them.

"*Es wird regnen,*" he said.

"I do not understand Afrikaans, baas," said Jacob, still looking up at the sky, and this was true, for most of his life so far he had spent in the native territories or in southern Natal.

"That is not Afrikaans, *dummkopf!* Did you never hear of Deutschland, of Germany?"

"No, baas."

"It is a great country which is far away from here."

"I have heard of England, baas."

"What has that to do with it? You will also hear of Germany, for I shall tell you. I shall tell you how powerful my country is and how great. What I said just now was that it is going to rain."

"Sometimes it rains, baas," said Jacob pleasantly but with a faint tone of indifference.

However, Hugo was paying no attention to him, and in a minute or two neither was paying attention to the other; Hugo went on talking about Germany and the new dawn in the world. If Jacob had looked then he would have seen tears in the eyes of the white baas, but he was staring at the sky. Presently Hugo's tears ran down his cheeks, and he had to stop talking, because he choked upon the words. There was a short interval of silence.

"*Hier bin ich zu lange geblieben,*" Hugo said.

"Yes, baas, it will rain," Jacob answered slowly.

"Stupid! I said I have remained here too long."

Yet he did not move, and Jacob said, "Tell me, baas, is it warm up there?"

Hugo saw that the black boy was still intent upon the sky, and he replied, "You were up there yourself, so you said. Then surely you must know whether it is warm."

"Yes, I was there, but I do not remember. It was all so quick."

Hugo gazed upward himself but found no solace. He saw nothing but the clouds drifting, the same clouds which made him think there would be rain. Impatiently he roused himself to action and ordered Jacob to produce food for breakfast. This was quickly done, and the two squatted and ate.

"But why do I eat?" Hugo asked himself. "I have nothing to live for. My soul is dead—my spirit is dead. I have killed them. Yet I am hungry, and I go on eating like an animal, no better than this disgusting black boy here. Is this just from habit, or is there still some further purpose? I think it is only habit."

He stood up and walked around to limber his legs and his body. The land to the east seemed to open abruptly into sky, with the Indian Ocean lying hazily in the distance. He went to the rim as Jacob had done the night before and looked over and down. His first sight filled him with awe and even made him giddy, but he was fascinated by the dropping of the mountain to the coast beneath, and he looked again earnestly.

"God in heaven!" he exclaimed then. "God in heaven!"

For a minute or two he could not move; he could not say anything more than this. The red roofs in the sun, the curve of the sandy beach, the muddy river flashing as it rippled past the jetty and over the spurs of sand. Then he found his tongue again.

"You, boy, come here! Is not that Port Quentin down there? Yes, it is. The place we went from, and here we are so close I could drop a stone into the streets. What kind of a guide are you? So you were leading me in a circle, and all those miles were for nothing at all! Speak up! What have you to say for yourself?"

Jacob stood mutely, and Hugo would have struck him if it had not been for his own struggle of conflicting impulses —the surprise of the discovery, disappointment, sudden fear and panic. Hugo cursed in German and then in English.

"But if the baas will look this way," said Jacob, motioning away from the break of the mountain and toward the back country, "he will see good things."

"Yes," said Hugo, "of course! The danger is not that way—it is right down below, looking up at us. Come, now, we will be making haste. I will not trust you any longer. I will be the commander, and you will take my orders, do you understand?"

As Hugo started away from the rim Jacob leaned out as far as he dared and then spat, but it did not go nearly into the town—it went only a little way and was lost in the green branches.

"I know why you played this trick upon me," Hugo said after they had gathered their belongings and started the new journey. "You wanted to follow that boy yesterday who was making the music. Well, now I know the kind you are, and I will watch you. I tell you it is a good thing I do not believe you guilty of real treachery, for if I did I would kill you."

Then as they walked on Hugo remembered that if Jacob had not turned aside so abruptly the day before they would have been overtaken by the automobile filled with Germans. At the time, of course, Hugo had run after the car, but that had been folly, for the purpose of a flight was to get away, and he would not so forget himself again, unless he decided to die, which was possible for anyone and more likely for some than for others. But as to the business of the day before, evidently when they had changed their direction to follow the boy with the concertina they had executed a piece of sound strategy. It had been a wise thing to double on their tracks and to spend the night on the heights overlooking Port Quentin, where no one would dream of seeking them. Hugo was surprised that he had not thought of this aspect of the matter at once.

"I am stupid," he told himself. "Perhaps the native boy has guile, but, whether he really has this gift of escape or not, without him I should certainly have been taken."

They were tramping upward, most of the time, but not always, following the winding roads, and resting from the hot sun in the shade of trees or sometimes in the shade of native huts. The rain came, but soon it stopped again, and they went on, drying themselves as they went.

Hugo had said that he was to be the commander, but there was no way he could command, since he was a stranger to the country and since the country mocked him.

He saw a bird hovering in the air and carrying behind it a long tail, almost like the tail of a kite. He watched with fascination, but the fascination was not pleasant, because here was one more of those strange things of the country, preventing him from getting back to a sense of proportion.

This was a pleasant, lazy land, but he did not know that. He looked for greater mysteries where there were none. The round hills again and again seemed lofty and terrifying, but they were actually gentle and civil, given over to the lives of the native tribes, to the grazing of cattle and small agriculture of a sort. There was order and law in the land, but these things were invisible, and Hugo suspected danger and violence behind the faces of black men who slept in the sun. There was always the strangeness, strangeness in every small thing from the feeling of the sunlight and the look of the bird with the long tail to the innumerable black faces. Often he closed his fingers on his automatic, but he realized that the menace of this secret countryside could not be ended with a bullet.

Jacob stood between him and the menace, although much of the time Jacob was part of the menace. They passed small trading posts, with little else but stores and broad expanses of bare red ground, and Hugo did not know that here some white couple lived in quietness, as likely as not with their children, just as families lived in tranquillity in German villages. They passed a miniature town with a street, two lines of buildings with galvanized-iron roofs, and a tiny hotel with a sign, "Union Beers," hanging from a spindling balcony. But even the sign failed to give

reassurance to Hugo. He saw it as only one more extrava-
gance, one more distortion in a land of hidden meaning.

The flight of Hugo and Jacob did not proceed in a
straight line or by logic or by any necessity, for Jacob
made up his geography as he went along and followed
the attractions of the countryside. Better than anything
else, Jacob loved to trek, and this trek filled him with
pleasure, for it was unhurried, and the sun was warm, and
the sky was filled, day after day, with droves of pleasant
white clouds. There was no labor, no monotonous repeti-
tion, no fixed and pressing duty—on the contrary, the singing air and the land beyond, day after day, bursting the
bonds not only of place but of time itself, for now the days
and the nights intermingled, and there was neither length
nor breadth, but only suspension in sunlit space, only the
quality of music heard in the open, leading and calling to
the soul.

When their first supply of provisions was used up it was
necessary for Jacob to forage for whatever he could get.
He traded with natives for bananas and mealies. Of water
there was no lack, for rain fell often enough, although in
brief downpours, and there were many pools and streams.
Hugo had in his pocket a single pound note, the allowance
of his own funds which he would have been permitted to
spend in South Africa. He had seen a fine stinkwood bowl
in a shop window in Port Quentin, a graceful bowl of a
pleasant roundness, the dark wood rich and deep in color,
unlike anything he had seen before. It had been his plan to
purchase this bowl to take home to Germany, but now he

looked at the note and thought of that plan sadly and of how youthfully and innocently he had formed it and how long ago it was. The last thing he needed in his present condition was a beautiful stinkwood bowl. Once, too, he had thought of buying something for Nicky, something that she would wear or keep in remembrance of him, close to her own warmth and sweetness. He smiled bitterly, gazing at the note as at something useless, because he could now purchase with it only the means of sustenance and safety, not some article to make negotiable in a mystic way the longing of his heart.

He gave the note to Jacob and told him to use it to buy food. But Jacob, when he went into a town or village, did not go to a store but hung about the back door of the hotel, scraping acquaintance with the servants and begging or bargaining for leftover scraps and such provisions as they would pilfer for him. He never paid more than a *tikkie* for anything, and so he kept a hoard of coins along with other bright objects—safety pins, buttons, and bits of glass—which he liked to collect upon his person.

Hugo wavered between the extremes of sharp suspicion and complete confidence in Jacob. He never questioned that the boy was a master of the secrets of the country, and when Jacob came back to him bearing food or walked with him past groups of staring natives he valued the services thus performed at far more than their real worth. At other times he wondered if Jacob might be plotting against him, even against his life. Even when he was most impressed with

Jacob's ability to manage the details of his journey he despised him for being black, dirty, and ignorant.

"It is I who am the commander," Hugo said to himself, "yet I am bound to rely upon this revolting creature. I have to yield myself and give in to him, because he knows the country and I do not. Yet the knowledge that he has is nothing more than the instinct which is born into a dog. He is not any better than an animal."

The time came when Hugo felt compelled to do something to assert his superiority and to establish what he felt to be the proper relationship between them.

"Since we must travel together," he said to Jacob, "this expedition must be conducted properly. I will show you how to stand at attention, and I will teach you some of the simple but important principles of military drill. Do you understand what I am saying?"

"Yes, baas," said Jacob.

"First you are to stand this way, arms at your sides, feet together, chin up. Every day there will be an inspection, after which I shall give you orders for the march."

Hugo cut a branch from a tree and trimmed it to make a staff with which Jacob could drill. He gave all his commands in German, and it was not long before Jacob could understand or at least recognize them.

"*Achtung!*" Hugo would command, and Jacob would come to a sort of attention, looking absurd in his greatcoat with the dangling braid.

"*Prasentirt das Gewehr! Gewehr auf die Schulter!*

Gewehr ab! Nein, nein! Why do you not understand such a simple thing? *Beim Fuss's Gewehr!*"

Or, again, Jacob would march up and down, turning squarely and stiffly, while Hugo stood and shouted at him.

"*Rechts um!*"

Jacob did not mind, for the exercises were of short duration and were not tiring. There was one part of the drill which Hugo showed him which occasionally he repeated by himself; it consisted of the stretching of the right arm stiffly forward and the uttering of the words, "Heil Hitler!" This amused Jacob, for it was a sort of play.

It seemed to Hugo that the journey was better arranged and that it went on more smoothly, yet he had no peace of mind. One day they came to a stream which was, for the most part, shallow, but with broad pools collected here and there behind rocky places and narrows. Here they rested, and, to his surprise, Hugo saw that Jacob had taken off his clothes and had thrown himself into the water, swimming and basking in the nearest pool. The black, lithe nakedness of the boy was not an unlovely thing to see. Jacob spread his arms and legs, swam slowly, then turned and flashed through the water, sending up shining drops.

Hugo envied Jacob, but he could not bring himself to swim in the same pool as the black boy. There were other pools, but some stubbornness in him kept him where he was; besides, he thought that he could not undress in front of Jacob, for this would not be becoming. Therefore he sat a little way from the bank and pretended not to notice what Jacob did in the water, although his own body ached

for the contact with the cool stream, and his muscles for
the relaxation of the pool in the sunlight.

They went on again, and all the while they seemed to be
climbing higher and higher, until at last the air was so clear
and so singing that they might have been close under the
sun. But at night the air turned cool. One afternoon there
were dark clouds in the sky, shouldering through a haze
which hurt the eyes. The clouds were heavy and did not
seem to move. At last there was lightning, and it appeared
to flash inside the clouds, illuminating them like lanterns,
instead of riving the sky as Hugo had watched the lightning
flashes at home. Under these flickering clouds they walked,
and the thunder rolled and rolled, but there was no rain,
and when the storm eventually subsided it seemed to have
moved no nearer and no farther than it had been in the
beginning.

The strangeness of the country lay upon Hugo strongly;
he was weary and, in a sense, afraid. He was like a person
in a dream, unable to escape. They were stopping then for
a rest, and he stood in his dusty, mud-caked uniform and
forced himself for the sake of something which had been
bred into him to utter commands.

"*Achtung!*"

Obediently Jacob slipped into the ritual, but when it was
over it had not helped Hugo to find balance or proportion
or peace. As he lay, trying to rest, his mind was teeming
with anxious thoughts.

Amid it all he asked himself, "What am I living for? I
know that life is not an end or a purpose in itself but only,

for some reason. I used to know the reason for my living, and I must get back to that, or I shall go mad. I am lost, but perhaps there is hope for redemption. Redemption must be what I am to strive for."

By redemption he meant one thing only, the thing shaped by past training and discipline and not influenced by this new country. His torment was somewhat relieved. But Jacob, resting on the ground, suffered from no torment at all.

11

THE LETTER which Nicky Birch addressed to Mr. Thomas Hickey of the Union Brewery was taken first by road motor service to Kokstad and then by train to Durban, where it was dispatched by plane as Nicky had intended. The air-mail service of the Union of South Africa had been highly developed, as became a country with an administrative capital and a legislative capital a thousand miles removed one from the other. Indeed, under some circumstances it had become necessary to write the word "surface" on a piece of mail if one wished it to be taken by land instead of by air.

Mr. Hickey happened at this time to be in Pretoria, in the regular course of his business, which required occasional conferences with government officials, so that after Nicky's letter reached Capetown it had to be flown another thousand miles over the scorching veld. So expeditiously was this rerouting accomplished that the letter was delivered to Mr. Hickey in Polley's Transvaal Hotel on Pretorious Street only five days after it had left Nicky's hand, and at a time when Hugo Becker and Jacob were pursuing their haphazard flight inland, with Hugo's mind somewhat fanatically fixed upon the idea of redemption.

There was a certain air of expectancy in Pretoria, but this had no relation to domestic affairs, which were humming along in peaceful prosperity, except for such hardy perennials as the native problem. The jacaranda trees had ceased blooming; the coming election was beginning to be proclaimed in posters which adjured city and country, Boer and Briton, to clasp hands, and the government was ready to move in a few weeks to Capetown for the opening of parliament. Certain members were arranging to twist the British lion's tail a bit by starting the parliamentary session off with the Afrikaans national anthem, *"Die Stem van Suid Afrika,"* as well as with the traditional "God Save the King." The newspapers were debating the purely academic question as to whether the Union would go to war in case Britain should take up arms again, but the issue was too remote for anything except political implications.

No, the air of expectancy had to do with none of these matters but solely with the expected birth of an infant to the Crown Princess Juliana and her husband, Prince Bernhard of Lippe Biesterfeld, in the far-off Netherlands. Against the day of the good news which it was hoped would arrive soon, the faggots had been piled high on a *kop* overlooking the city, and torches were in readiness to touch off a bonfire of glad celebration. No one could yet imagine, even in a nightmare, that this baby about to be born into a peaceful world would in a little more than two years be a fugitive on alien soil. That bad dream was in the making, but it had not begun to rise out of the black pool.

Mr. Hickey had been intending to prolong his stay in Pretoria so that he might witness the spectacle of the great bonfire, but Nicky's letter gave him something more practical to think about, and he was nothing if not a practical man. One of his most conspicuous attributes was an intuitive knowledge of what to do with inside information. He did not attach any weight to Nicky's purpose in writing, which seemed to him a foolish purpose, though one natural in a nice girl and very appealing. She implored him to have an eye out for this young German and to befriend him in all possible ways—also, Mr. Hickey gathered, in impossible ways, which was understandable and just like a sentimental girl. His own viewpoint left no room for such nonsense, but he saw no inconsistency in pursuing his notion of the real issue and at the same time leading Nicky on so that he and she might have some jolly times together.

One of the things about Mr. Hickey which made him valuable to his employers was that he invariably knew the right man to see about anything, no matter how unusual or how questionable its nature, and if, by any chance, he did not know at the moment he was quick to find out. He was never to be seen floundering or making false motions, and he never left tracks. In short, he was a born politician and had a flair for intrigue, and there had never been a better opportunity for the use of his talents. Up to now he had not taken on anything of an international character, but he knew where to find the ministries of foreign nations on the tree-shaded streets of Pretoria, and within a couple of hours he had made an appointment with Dr. Karl Weiss, who, he was assured, was exactly the man to handle such an affair.

He met Dr. Weiss at the zoo and had no trouble at all in picking him out. The doctor was approaching middle age, but he had a youngish gait and a rather dandified appearance; his hair was thinning, and his gray eyes did not seem particularly strong, for he wiped them occasionally with his handkerchief and habitually lowered and narrowed his brows as if to give them aid. His chin was pointed, but at the end it was hollowed with an extremely large dimple. Notwithstanding these items, which individually were odd or not particularly attractive, Dr. Weiss on the whole made a dignified, almost professional impression, with a carefully aloof but not inconsiderate manner. He was somewhat taller than Mr. Hickey, but no more powerfully built, and he seemed to be slipping over into the ripeness of sedentary life.

Before Dr. Weiss and Mr. Hickey said anything much they looked at the elephants for a while and then walked past most of the other animals, as if they had come for this purpose and for no other. Mr. Hickey was impatient, but he knew better than to try to force the situation. At last, to his great relief, Dr. Weiss suggested that they be seated on a bench near a fringe of trees.

"This is," he said, "a most beautiful park, is it not? I see there is no one else about." Then, without a change in the even expression of his voice, he went on, "I want you to understand that I have no connection whatever with the German government, no connection whatever. I trust that this is quite clear?"

"Yes, of course," said Mr. Hickey. "I see."

"Very well, then. I hope there will not be any doubt about this important matter at any time."

"You can depend on me," said Mr. Hickey. "Now this is what I've got hold of. It is concerning a certain chap who deserted from that battleship down at Port Quentin."

Dr. Weiss continued to stare into the trees a little distance away as he inquired, "Is that the substance of what you are intending to tell me?"

Mr. Hickey was quick to appreciate the noncommittal note in the doctor's attitude, and he replied quickly, "Heard about that, did you? Well, that's only the start-off."

"It happens," said Dr. Weiss, "that I keep myself somewhat well informed of current events. Some of us are like that, you know. I think in me it is the scientific attitude." He smiled, and when his lips were parted in this way they looked broad and shiny. "By the way, Mr. Hickey, I think we may agree on one other point of understanding which will save time and difficulty in the future. What you have said is not something which should be widely repeated, or,

in fact, repeated at all. Let us simply say that there is a
Mr. Smith who is said to be making a little tour in this
country, and let us say that—for purely personal reasons—
I am desirous of learning anything of consequence which
relates to this Mr. Smith."

"I follow you, Dr. Weiss," said Mr. Hickey. "You can
be sure of that, and I don't mind saying that you're the
type of man I like to have a conversation with. We'll get
on, we will. Now as to this Mr. Smith, I've had a letter in
regards to him, a personal letter, you understand, which I
am not at liberty to allow anyone to read, but it gives some
information. . . ."

Mr. Hickey let his voice come slowly to a stop and began
to light a cigar. His eyes were narrowed, and they were
fixed inquiringly upon Dr. Weiss.

"You can inform me where Mr. Smith is?"

"No, not exactly. Not this minute, at least."

"Well?"

"I know who he's with," said Mr. Hickey.

"So!" said Dr. Weiss.

"Yes, I've got quite a description, and, drawing one or
two conclusions which won't be far wrong, I've got a very
good—oh, an excellent—notion of where to look for Mr.
Smith himself. He'll be surprised, he will!"

"That is very interesting. I will be frank with you. It
is very interesting indeed. Shall we summarize this information and discuss your conclusions without further loss of
time?"

"There's just one thing," said Mr. Hickey.

"Yes."

"I want to know where I come in. No offense, I hope, but, you being just a private citizen—no connection with any government, you see . . . The point to some information is that it's valuable, or should be."

"I understand your feeling. You know, of course, through what channel you communicated with me? You do, yes, naturally! Then I take it you will appreciate my responsibility in such matters, even as a private citizen. The answer to your question as to where you come in, Mr. Hickey, is that you will come in according to the value of your assistance to me. For the present I can say only that you will, of course, be relieved of all expense."

Mr. Hickey drew upon his cigar and let the smoke drift out slowly from his pursed lips.

"I see," he said at last. "I see, and it's good enough, it is. Good enough. No more beating about the bush now. Here's what I know, and then I'll tell you what I deduce from the facts."

Mr. Hickey leaned forward and repeated to Dr. Weiss certain passages from Nicky's letter, almost verbatim, since he had studied them well. He placed greatest importance upon a description of Jacob, for the description was a vivid one; plainly Nicky had given it because it supplied the most promising chance for anyone to establish contact with Hugo. Mr. Hickey did not miss any of the significance, and he was satisfied to observe that Dr. Weiss was just as favorably impressed. He went on to explain that the mysterious Mr. Smith was certainly not making for any port on the coast; no, he was making for the interior, and he could not be moving any great distance in a day, because he was on foot, and the country was not easy, especially for someone who had to keep more or less out of sight.

"There are," concluded Mr. Hickey, "only just so many places where this Mr. Smith can be coming up."

"There is no doubt as to the reliability of your informant?" asked Dr. Weiss.

"Not the least," said Mr. Hickey. "She's—— What I mean is, he's an unsuspecting sort that doesn't have an idea of what he's giving away."

"I had been led to believe," said Dr. Weiss, "as the result of certain reports, of certain appearances, and some steps that were taken, that Mr. Smith was probably in hiding, perhaps in a prepared place of concealment."

"It doesn't look like it," said Mr. Hickey.

"I hope you are correct."

"But there wouldn't be any place this chap could go, unless he had help. . . . Oh, I see what the game is. It's deeper than it looks. I took it for an ordinary bolt, but there's more to it, after all. Well!"

Dr. Weiss said nothing for a minute or two, and Mr. Hickey's quick mind ran over the possibilities for him, and they seemed to be improving. If the Germans suspected that Hugo Becker's flight was well planned and that he might have accomplices, then there was a real plot in back of it all. Perhaps there were British agents working against the German agents, and in that case he had got onto something important. He felt like whistling.

"As an experienced man, Mr. Hickey," said Dr. Weiss, "you are aware that events usually happen according to plan or for some serious purpose. Events of a certain type, that is. It is just as well you should realize this, because your discretion will then be greater. But I suggest that we avoid any needless speculation and confine ourselves to Mr. Smith. You were going to propose something?"

"I was thinking I might take my car and do a bit of investigating. I could do it, you see, without anybody looking at me twice, and, since I know all the hotels through having called on them many times about Union beers, it wouldn't be long before I picked up something. Then I could let you know."

"It is a good suggestion, except for one thing," said Dr. Weiss. "I myself will go with you. The matter, as I have told you, is an interesting one, and no time should be lost."

"Glad to have you, of course," Mr. Hickey said, but his voice dragged a little, and in a moment he went on, "You aren't coming along because you don't have confidence in me, I hope?"

"What reason have I for lacking confidence in you, Mr. Hickey?" asked Dr. Weiss blandly, with his shiny lips parted in a smile.

"None at all."

"Exactly!"

They both laughed loudly, like old friends, but Mr. Hickey did not see what was funny. The thing that bothered him was the part of his plan which he had not divulged to Dr. Weiss, the part which concerned Nicky. He had expected to go shooting off alone and to have Nicky join him and to combine pleasure with the eventual profit of turning Hugo Becker over to the Germans. Now it was not quite clear how he was to have his chance with Nicky, but his determination to have it had not diminished.

"How soon do you want to start?" he asked Dr. Weiss.

"In an hour, if you can be ready."

Mr. Hickey's eyebrows went up, and he looked at the doctor with some astonishment.

"You do mean business, don't you? Well, you can count on me every time. In an hour it is! You just be at Polley's, and you will find me ready for you."

Back in his hotel room, packing, Mr. Hickey kept sitting down on the bed to think. Everything had gone well for him so far, yet for some reason he was dissatisfied; he felt as if he were being hurried along by some superior force, like a small child held by the scruff of the neck. Not that it should make much difference if old boy Weiss wanted to come along . . . except in one particular.

"Well, it's still my show," mumbled Mr. Hickey to nobody at all, and he sat down once more to write a note to Nicky. He assured her of his warm interest in anything which was near her heart and suggested that if she could arrange to meet him at a place which he would presently be in a position to designate he was certain he could show her something to her advantage.

"You had best start directly you receive this," he went on, "and be careful not to let anyone know what you are about. Proceed as far as Umtata and put up at the Royal Hotel, where I will communicate with you by telegraph. If you are followed you know what will happen, so I advise you to come alone."

He signed the letter, "Yours to command, Thomas Hickey."

When this was done he smiled at himself in the mirror with a disingenuous widening of his eyes, as if he, too, were among those who should be deceived by the cleverness of Thomas Hickey. The trouble was that there was still an uneasiness in the back of his mind; Nicky would come, all right, if he knew anything about women, but how was he going to keep Dr. Weiss from getting too nosy and too suspicious? He sighed and told himself he would just have to cross that bridge when he came to it. He fancied it would not be pleasant to have Dr. Weiss doubting his good faith.

12

Hʊɢᴏ ᴀɴᴅ ᴊᴀᴄᴏʙ were pursued. They had been skirting a small settlement, and suddenly they heard yells and turned to see two men, evidently white men, running toward them along the hillside. Hugo took to his heels, calling to Jacob to keep up with him. It might have been that the two men wanted to ask some question, but Hugo did not even think of this possibility until later. One pursuit could not differ from another so long as he was a fugitive, and he ran first and reflected later. He did not know where the men came from, and he hardly glanced back until he and Jacob were out of their sight and ready to throw themselves into a donga. They stayed in the donga for a long time and were close together.

Jacob sat with his knees under his chin, clasping his legs with his arms, and Hugo lay almost at full length. It occurred to Hugo that this would be a good time for him to learn more about South Africa, but he could not bring himself to question the black boy or to talk with him at all. Instead he kept sullenly silent, thinking what shame had come to him and wishing he could order Jacob to leave the place and get out of his sight. After a while, however, Jacob began to talk of his own choice, and Hugo listened in spite of himself.

Jacob began to tell about the white princess who lived in the treetop and about the elephant which pulled upon a strange rope of vines and raised the princess and her warriors into the treetop at incredible speed. He described various animals of the jungle and endowed them with human attributes and implied that he could converse with them whenever he chose. This was all drawn from his one most fascinating source, the Tarzan motion picture, but it was not consecutive, and some things he rejected and others he dwelt upon with fondness.

Hugo said at last, "I think you lie. I think you lie most stupidly."

"No, baas," said Jacob, "I do not lie."

And it was true that he did not lie, for he never meant to misrepresent reality; reality was one thing, and truth was another. Or perhaps there were different kinds of truth, and the one he liked best was a sort of art, a thing of the mind, which added to an individual's self-respect and enlarged his world. This art, too, was real in its own way. What he had seen he had seen, and what he had heard he had heard, although he did not for a moment expect those adventures to be translated or repeated in the actual region of experience which lay across the shadow line.

"Well," said Hugo, relenting, to his own surprise, "if you do not lie, at least I cannot understand what you are talking about."

When daylight was almost gone they climbed out of the donga and brushed the yellow-red dust from their clothes. Jacob led the way, and they went then to a circle of native huts at no great distance and concealed themselves there. Hugo saw the black chief first in the dusk, a tall, thin man with sunken cheeks and anxious eyes, ribs showing through his taut skin. There were also many women, naked to the waist, and small children running about like animals but with an air of happiness which animals lack. Hugo's knowledge of undressed women was meager, and when the chief's wives, innocent of what is known as modesty, gathered around to look at him he was flushed with embarrassment. He was glad when the opportunity came to sleep.

The next day, while Hugo hid, a sight-seeing bus came out from some city or town, and he could hear the tourists talking as they took photographs and peered at the natives and at the wattle-and-daub huts. He had been prepared for nothing like this, and the voices of the white people had the strangest of effects upon him. It was as if he were suspended or confined in open space, detached from the world, in a waking dream. He lay at the fringe of civilization, but he could not reach out his hand; he could not cry out a greeting.

There was a woman's voice, and after he had heard it a minute or two he began to think of Nicky and to yearn for her. Not that the voice was like Nicky's; it was not, but it was clear, gentle, and feminine. It penetrated his concealment; it entered his ears; it caught him disarmed. The presence of Nicky seemed to come to him, and he wanted to call upon her for help and to tell her that he had not meant to blame her for his flight or to hate her for her part in it. He wanted to rise up and find Nicky and take her in his arms and feel her hair and her smooth cheek against his tired face. He called out to Nicky, without words and without voice, and there was no answer.

He crawled on his hands and knees and peeped through a slit in the wall of a hut. The woman whose tongue had moved him so was skinny and ugly. She had a smug hatchet face. He felt betrayed. The presence of Nicky was gone, and so was his flood of feeling for her.

After a while the tourists gave tips and cigarettes to the chief and some of the others and climbed into the bus and were driven away again. All this time the chief had been naked and glistening black except for some beads around his neck and feathered strips dangling from a cord about his waist, but when the tourists had gone Hugo saw him step around in back of his hut and pull on a pair of trousers.

The effect of this trifling incident upon Hugo was out of all proportion to its importance. He did not like to see a cheat put upon the white people by the black, and he was uncomfortably aware that he did not himself know what was real and what was sham. Again the country mocked

him, and the natives mocked him, and there was nothing he
could do about it except stew and hate.

Jacob offered Hugo some cigarettes the white tourists
had brought, and Hugo rejected the offer with furious
anger, but a few minutes later he relented and took the
cigarettes, because he was possessed of a desire to smoke
which was so strong that everything else went down before
it. He lighted one (they were Springboks, a popular South
African brand), and there was something so enjoyable and
luxurious about it that he was almost in ecstasy. It was a
long time since he had held a cigarette in his hand. But in
spite of the satisfaction, he was in his own mind dishonored
and degraded more than he had been before. He lay on
the ground and smoked away his pride, his self-esteem, and
the more he did so the more he was determined to be redeemed. He became hard and single-minded for redemption.

As he lay there, keeping his thoughts away, he heard
Jacob and the black chief conversing.

"You have come far?" the chief inquired.

"Forty days' journey," replied Jacob, who had no sense
of time and chose a round number at random.

"That is far. How much is before you and the white
baas?"

"A hundred days," said Jacob.

The chief seemed impressed. After a minute he asked,
"How do you like trekking with the white baas?"

"It is good," said Jacob, "except for one thing. I do not
like the smell of the white baas."

Hugo rose from the ground as if he had been struck with a stick and then restrained himself, quivering with indignation and rage. This was more than a slight, a dishonor put upon him and his white manhood—it was the discovery of a scandalous point of view, a minority report upon his race which should be put down with the kind of chastisement such impudence deserved. A black boy had no right to think such a thing. Hugo felt the presence of a creeping, abhorrent animal world upon which he needed to put his foot. That is what he would do one day. He would come through his ordeal, strengthened by hot sun and inner flame, to strike out and prove his place among men. Not until long afterward did he recall that once he had read about animals having characteristic scents and think that perhaps human creatures had them also, and what is pleasant to one may not be pleasant to another.

As soon as the sun was past its peak Hugo and Jacob started on again, directing their steps still inland, still, for the most part, up toward the hills higher even than those they had already passed. Now that they had been pursued it seemed to Hugo that some understanding should be reached in case they should be separated by any sudden chance. He ought to have thought of such a contingency before, since Jacob had gone off alone so frequently on foraging trips, and Hugo might easily have had to change his hiding place before the black boy returned. What was needed, as a wise precaution, was an agreement upon some rendezvous to which both he and Jacob would repair.

The next day they were near a village, and Hugo ordered

Jacob to go into this village and to the office of the road motor service.

"You must do exactly as I tell you," he said, "for nothing is more important than this. You must buy the timetables, a book with a map in it, for which you will pay a shilling, and you must not say you are buying it for your baas. Say what you like, but not that. Do you understand?"

"Yes, baas," said Jacob.

Then Jacob went into the town, which was a small place called Kirk, and found the road motor office. He proffered a shilling for the timetables, and the man at the window looked at him curiously.

"It is for the baas," said Jacob, because that was what one always said, and not to say it, or to say anything else instead, would have been a reversal of all custom.

When Jacob had returned with the book Hugo took the map and spread it out before him. He had learned from Jacob the name of the town.

"Now I see where we are!" he exclaimed. "Now I can make a plan. This is what I should have had from the beginning. We have come crookedly, due to you and your foolishness. But I do not blame you, because I know you have guile in throwing off pursuit. You are wise in the secrets of the country, but you have no military sense."

It was Hugo's idea that he should make for the mountains where he and Jacob could remain in hiding for a while, until there was no acute danger left. He imagined that there would be plenty of game, and Jacob could shoot enough to keep them supplied as long as necessary. He studied the map and was attracted by the name of what appeared to be a small town, Lady Elsie, perhaps seventy or eighty miles from Kirk. To reach this place they would cross the railroad once, leave it again for a climb through what was apparently mountainous country, and join it finally at Lady Elsie, their destination. As nearly as Hugo could judge, there was likely to be no better retreat for one in his circumstances, and he began to explain the plan to Jacob.

"Look!" he said, his finger pointing to Lady Elsie on the map. "This is where we are to go. It will not require many days more, do you see? The town is called Lady Elsie. Do you know the place? Well, it does not matter. But you must remember that if you do not find me or if I do not find you we are to meet there. Do you understand? Good. I do not care now if we become separated, because if we are not seen together there will be so much more difficulty in tracing us. That is a good idea. And remember this, too: if we finish the journey separately the one who reaches Lady Elsie first is to keep a sharp lookout for the other."

"Yes, baas," said Jacob, and in a way he understood. He was quite clear about the name of their destination, but conditional matters were of no great concern to him, and he did not count upon being separated from Hugo.

A few hours later the separation, however, took place. They had come to the railroad line, and during Jacob's absence after food Hugo thought it wise to avoid some railroad workers. He said to himself that it would be a relief to be rid of Jacob for a while; he would feel cleaner and more like himself. He was soon striking off on his own toward Lady Elsie, hungry but with a certain new satisfaction. Jacob, returning to the place where he had left the baas, did not find him.

Jacob frowned, for there was one great difficulty. It was true that he loved to trek, but trekking was an object in itself. As to destination, that was seldom definite—he usually headed for regions in general, and he liked to follow his fancy, the sun, and the wind, the inviting ways. How to go *to* some specific spot where he had never been before, as an assigned duty, was perplexing. Which road should he follow? He had looked at a piece of paper in Hugo's hand, but that meant nothing to him as to north, east, or west, or as to the look of the countryside. The problem was insoluble, unless . . . unless . . .

Jacob walked back to Kirk and went to the office of the road motor service and asked for a ticket to Lady Elsie. The man at the window seemed doubtful, but Jacob said his baas had given him the order. Then the man explained that it would be necessary to take the road-motor coach to Empton and then to take the train from Empton to Tarleton East, and then to take the road motor coach from Tarleton East to Lady Elsie. The matter was complicated, but Jacob knew about tickets and that all he had to do was to show them. What was left of Hugo's money, except for a few tikkies, went to pay for the passage.

Then, since the coach ran only three times a week, Jacob loitered about the rear entrance of the hotel in Kirk and made an impression upon the black servants by giving them the "Heil Hitler" salute which none of them had ever seen. He told them stories, and they gave him food to eat, and then he slept long and comfortably.

Hugo, meantime, was toiling onward alone, keeping his bearings by the sun, sleeping during the heat of the day, and walking long after dark. The hills were no longer smooth and round; he came to the broken mountains, rugged and gleaming brown or red, with krantzes furrowing their sides and making designs of light and shade. He came into the country of strange rocky pinnacles and towers, fantastic as sculptured figures. They were pitted and eroded by time, and some were bulbous with eroded necks supporting them. They frowned like titanic faces, distorted, and Hugo was afraid.

One day he met a small native boy in a stretch of wild country, and the boy carried three speckled trout. Hugo traded two cigarettes, which he had hoarded, for one of the fish and then cooked it over an open fire. The most tedious and onerous part of the journey was the climb over Tarleton Pass, winding among the lofty mountains, up and up and up and then, at last, slowly down again. Sometimes he thought he would die before ever he managed to reach Lady Elsie. Sometimes when his thoughts ran themselves almost into a fever he pretended that he was journeying to the Rhine and that he would before too long arrive at that symbolic river instead of at a strange South African village.

Jacob, meantime, had found his journey by coach and rail a considerable delight. He relished the magic and power by which he was transported swiftly, and he sat up straight and looked with friendliness at the mountains which unrolled themselves before his eyes without any exertion on his part. In the towns he saw the pleasant steeples of churches, the balconied hotels; he saw lawns and schools and libraries. Hugo's trek was through a hostile land, wild, with countless imagined enemies. Jacob's was through a decent region of long-accustomed country life, with grazing sheep and cattle and the thin, assured stir of commerce.

When he reached Tarleton Pass Jacob listened with satisfaction to the grinding of the coach motor in low gear, and he was pleased with the sensation of height. He took this easy surmounting of the mountain barrier as something entirely matter-of-course.

Lady Elsie was built in a sort of horseshoe formed by the mountains. More than a mile above the sea level it stood, basking in the high air which was hot by day and cool by night. Hugo followed the road as far as he dared and then hid himself until darkness had fallen. Late at night he approached the village, marked in the starlight by church steeples and by a few glowing windows. When he had come quite close he hesitated and walked about, exploring, advancing in one direction after another, then retreating again. Finally he heard Jacob's voice.

"Baas! It is I, Jacob!"

Jacob led Hugo to a place near the railroad tracks where there was an angular shelter of galvanized iron once used by workers on the railway. Jacob had pulled the shelter aside into a border of trees and rough terrain where it could not be seen and had put brush in front. Since the night was clear, they did not go under the shelter but lay beside it, and Hugo gazed with astonishment at Jacob, who, as well as he could make out in the poor light, was not travel-worn at all.

"I am at the point of death with weariness," Hugo said to himself, "but he—look at him! He has not minded the hard journey, that is certain. I do not understand it." Then, aloud, he inquired, "When did you arrive here?"

Jacob shrugged.

"Have you been here a day?"

"Yes, baas."

"Two days?"

"Yes, baas."

"God in heaven!" ejaculated Hugo. "Of what is this black boy made?"

After Hugo had slept for a time he woke and lay quietly, reflecting that here the first phase of the journey into exile had ended. He had completed a labor of Hercules, and here, surely, he would be safe. Here he would form his plans for a return to the things he had lost, for the regaining of his own soul.

At that particular time Mr. Hickey and Dr. Weiss, with less exercise of sagacity than they had expected would be required of them, had come upon the broad trail left by Jacob in the course of his coach-train-and-coach journey from Kirk to Lady Elsie. Jacob in his big coat, telling stories to kitchen boys in hotels, begging food, referring to his mysterious baas; Jacob en route, transferring, loitering at stations, inviting the attention of all mankind. Dr. Weiss had even been informed, through the shrewd offices of Mr. Hickey, concerning the incident of the Nazi salute and the black boys at the hotel in Kirk, and he could not help showing his amazement.

"That's a sticker, that one is," observed Mr. Hickey with satisfaction.

But Mr. Hickey was having his troubles. He had dispatched a telegram to Nicky at the Royal Hotel, Umtata, bidding her meet him as soon as possible at Lady Elsie but not to let on that she knew him until he gave the word. As to the telegram itself, Mr. Hickey felt immensely satisfied, but he had an uncomfortable feeling that Dr. Weiss knew he had sent it. How the doctor had found out was beyond his imagining, for he had handled the piece of disingenuous business with his customary care.

"Unless he has eyes in the back of his German head," said Mr. Hickey to himself.

Perhaps it had been a mistake not to be frank with the doctor concerning Nicky, for this was an affair which was not to interfere with the main business transaction, but it was too late for frankness now. Mr. Hickey knew he was going to play matters double, and no harm done—but he did wish that Dr. Weiss would not look at him with that brassy look in those peculiar eyes.

13

Now that they were in residence, so to speak, Hugo thought it was high time he sent Jacob to do some hunting. He hungered for fresh food, especially meat. All around were the mountains, the first really hopeful aspect of this country he had seen—serried, spreading mountains, with peaks far off against the sky. Among them ran green valleys and furrows which surely suggested game. Hugo's first plan had been to withdraw deep into the mountains to make a camp, but the spot Jacob had chosen seemed suitable. There was an advantage in being near the town, and this was certainly not too near.

Lady Elsie seemed to be a small place, apparently of not more than a thousand inhabitants. It was off by itself, and there would be no passing through. Evidently the chief occupation was the grazing of cattle, for Hugo had seen a number of herds, all some distance away. Everything about the outlook was reassuring, and Hugo thought that he must have Jacob procure him a suit of civilian clothes, and that, so dressed, he might venture into the town to learn the latest news and to judge for himself how long he should remain hidden and what his next step should be. But first Jacob must hunt.

Hugo was lying on the ground near the improvised tent of galvanized iron, the morning sunlight falling warmly upon his face.

"Boy!" he called out sharply. "*Achtung!*"

Jacob emerged from the shelter slowly, wiping his eyes, and stood at attention.

"Is it true that you are a mighty hunter?"

"Oh yes, baas!" replied Jacob with a bright smile and a flash of his teeth.

"Good! You shall have a chance to show what you can do. Have you ever seen a pistol like this? Watch, and I will show you how it works. See? Take it and go where the game is, but be careful not to waste ammunition, do you understand? You must kill what you are aiming at with your first shot."

Jacob took the pistol and held it gingerly, letting the sunlight flash from the polished steel.

"Tomorrow, baas?"

"No," said Hugo, "today. Get fresh meat, do you understand? I am dying for fresh meat. And guard that pistol carefully, because I have not let it out of my hands before. Well, what are you waiting for?"

Obediently Jacob set out on his mission and was soon lost to Hugo's sight among the hillocks and ridges. He continued to hold the pistol in his hand with a tight grip, for this was the first time he had ever had any sort of fire-arm in his possession. He was afraid of the thing and carried it awkwardly. The mountains loomed ahead, and he went toward them, but the heaps of broken stone and rubble made walking difficult, and the rocky faces above seemed unfriendly. The only trail or path was an occasional track made by cattle, and these led nowhere in particular. Long, irregular crevices were filled with vegetation, lining and garnishing the mountains, but, for the most part, they were stark and bare. In the sunlight the rock warmed with color, and the krantzes glistened, but in the shadow the rock was cold and secret.

Jacob stood gazing, and finally he began to scramble upward along one of the seams. When this way became difficult he slid across to another and continued climbing for almost an hour before he found himself at the top of a ridge. He sat and surveyed the view with considerable interest, especially Lady Elsie, a toy village over yonder, with mountains in the background as far as he could see. But there were also mountains behind the ridge where he sat, immediate mountains, stretching their rock surfaces so high that he did not care to think about them. The only part of the scenery which attracted him was the village, and that attracted him greatly.

Except for a bird hopping about in the foliage of some small clinging bushes, there appeared to be no animal life.

However, some curiosity and perhaps a faint shadow of
hope prompted Jacob to hold the pistol at arm's length
and to press the trigger. Nothing happened, because he had
not understood Hugo's instructions as to handling the automatic. Jacob examined the pistol, tried it a few times more,
and began to feel an indifference toward it, even a kind of
contempt. He put it into his pocket. His perch on the ridge
was not comfortable for a long stay, and presently he
began to clamber down, making the descent in a short time,
at the cost of several rips in his greatcoat. One of these rips
soon lengthened and divided the coat in the rear from top
to bottom.

Jacob knew that he must get meat, and without any
further thought he walked as rapidly as possible to Lady
Elsie and strolled into the town. Nobody paid much attention to him, for there was a large native population in the
district. On either side were the brown-baked stucco buildings with awnings over the sidewalks, and at the head of
the principal street stood a Wesleyan church, across from
it the Royal Hotel. The hotel took Jacob's eye. It stood a
little back from the street, with a cement wall bordering a
small lawn. The building itself had only one story, but
there were covered platforms along two sides.

Jacob went around to the rear where there was a considerable space devoted to the work of the establishment.
The ground was hard and baked, except for odd corners
where grass grew among the cartons and barrels deposited
there. Between the hotel and the back street was a galvanized-iron garage which also bore the painted inscription,

"Sample Room." Here the ground sloped gently upward, and the back street was not cut through, so that a screen of shambling trees up above gave a kind of protection to the Royal's exposed rear.

In a little while Jacob had found an impressionable black boy named Tennis who worked as a porter and general servant and told Tennis some stories about his baas who, he said, was on the way to rescue a white princess who lived in a treetop. He showed Tennis the pistol, and by this time there were other native boys gathered around in admiration. When Jacob saw how things were going it occurred to him to trade the pistol for what he could get, and he went about the matter deviously and earnestly, with the benefit of considerable past experience which extended back into his earliest youth.

When the trade was completed Jacob had given up the pistol and his greatcoat, for which he no longer cared, in view of the tears, in exchange for a hotel porter's khaki tunic and shorts, a soiled red fez, a leather dispatch case with a broken strap which had been mended with twine, and a quarter of beef abstracted from the hotel stores. His new costume transformed him completely, for his naturally slim and well-proportioned figure was now apparent.

It was necessary for him to conceal himself until after dark, because the quarter of beef was hard to carry, and he did not care to be seen with it as he went out of town. He spent the rest of the day comfortably, and when the time seemed appropriate he roused and struck out for the spot where Hugo was hidden, reaching it without misadventure.

Hugo was sitting near the iron tent, waiting with impatience and some distress of mind, for he had been expecting Jacob's return long before this.

"Is it you?" he called. "What has happened?"

Jacob came closer and deposited the beef upon the ground.

Hugo could see indistinctly in the dim light of the stars and the small moon, and he leaned forward and felt the meat eagerly with his hands. It had been warmed considerably through the day.

"This is good!" he exclaimed. "This is very good! What have you shot? What kind of a creature is this?"

"Big," said Jacob after a brief hesitation. "Big animal, baas."

In his joy and satisfaction Hugo did not question that Jacob had shot some antelope or zebra or whatever the creature might have been. He supposed, without really thinking of the matter closely, that Jacob had been compelled to leave the rest of the carcass.

No less pleased, Jacob squatted in comfort and began to tell, in a singsong voice, the story of his hunt, the perils he had braved, and how he had brought down the mighty creature of the mountain, but just what kind of animal it was he could not make up his mind, or, at any rate, did not say. Meantime Hugo, his mouth watering, was cutting generous slices from the beef. He built a small fire where it could not be seen from outside the sheltering vegetation, and presently he was broiling the meat and relishing its pleasant odor as it browned and dripped in the flame.

Jacob's voice lost all meaning, except that it was a kind of intonation and an accompaniment for the preparation of the feast.

Hugo and Jacob both ate with gusto, holding the meat in their fingers. The night around them was cool and delicious, and they both were young.

But in the morning, when the sun had risen, Hugo looked at the quarter of beef from which he had cut the slices, and fury began to possess him.

"Why have you lied to me?" he demanded of Jacob. "You did not kill this animal. It has been dead a great while, and I believe it is no more than an ordinary cow slaughtered in the market."

"Some magic has changed it during the night, baas," Jacob suggested faintly, backing away as Hugo came toward him.

"I will teach you not to tell me such lies," said Hugo, and struck at the black boy but did not quite reach him. He cried out angrily, "Stop where you are! *Achtung!* Where is my pistol?"

"I do not know where it is, baas," said Jacob, standing his ground for the moment.

"What! You not only lie but you betray me. The truth is that you have sold my pistol to get yourself those new clothes. Speak now! Is not that the truth?"

"Yes, baas," said Jacob.

Jacob stood there, not strictly at attention but in an attitude somewhat approaching that in which he had been trained, and Hugo stepped up to him quickly and struck him, knocking him to the ground. Then Hugo kicked him twice.

"That will teach you," he said. "That will teach you."

Hugo was glad he had struck and kicked the black boy. He was glad in a way he had never known before, but it was a way he recognized as being creditable and much honored among men who deserved glory for deeds, not words. He was in a pattern which he would have set for himself, had he known how to rise to this exaltation. He was being hard and sure and firm—just too. This was the course prescribed for those upon whom Nazi Germany relied to carry her forward to the greatness which was rightly hers. No weakness, no inaction, no tolerance of treachery and cowardice. Hugo did not think of all this in words at the moment; he was simply glad in that certain way, and his gladness meant all the rest, and he was aware of it without any necessity for thinking.

"Now get up. I tell you get up!" he said to Jacob. "You will listen to your orders for today, and see that you carry them out. You have fitted yourself in new clothes—see that you do the same for me. It is necessary that I have a coat and trousers, do you understand? I will tell you again, slowly, so that there will not be any mistake." He repeated the instructions in his hard, pitiless voice and added, "If you know what is good for you you will not betray me again. Now go. Do you hear? Go."

Jacob rose from the ground, his right leg showing red where it had been scraped against the gravel. Without speaking he looked at Hugo with pain and surprise and then got away as fast as he could.

When he had gone Hugo said to himself, "I should have done that long before. If I did not feel so happy and confident now I should despise myself because I have been so weak until today. But all that is past, and I will not be weak any more. I am beginning to understand what there is for me to do."

He walked about for a few minutes and then sat down, drawing designs in the sand with a stick while he was busy with his thoughts. He heard the sound of someone approaching and thought that Jacob was coming back. He looked up angrily, ready for another outburst of his newly realized mastery. The brush parted at the entrance to the camping place.

"What do you want now?" he demanded. "I told you to go."

There was no answer, but as he looked he saw Nicky Birch appear within the rough enclosure. She stood on the other side looking at him. She wore no hat, and her yellow-brown hair was blown about her face. It was as if she had just stepped in from a country home in the neighborhood.

14

JULIE WILLIAMS and Nicky Birch drove into Lady Elsie that morning after an impetuous journey from Umtata, somewhat hampered by local showers and bad places in the road. The whole distance was less than two hundred miles, and they had planned to complete it on the day before. However, the obstacles had proved too great, and they had spent the night at a village this side of Kirk, making a start when the sun was just over the horizon. To Nicky, who had traveled little, the expedition itself was exciting, especially after several days of enforced inactivity in the heat of Umtata, where they had waited for Mr. Hickey's telegram, according to the explicit instructions contained in his letter to Nicky which he had written from Pretoria.

The letter came to her in Port Quentin as a spark which

could not fail to kindle a fire, and the fire was her eagerness, her hope, and the rapid beating of her heart. She had
no quarrel with Mr. Hickey's quaint expressions, for all
that mattered was the fact of going to Hugo, at once, without delay. She had to have help, however, and she con-
fided in Julie.

"But," said Julie, "what do you know of this man
Hickey? He sounds rather awful, don't you think?"

"What does it matter?" asked Nicky.

And then, to Nicky's surprise, Julie said, "Perhaps not
so very much. I will go with you. We will take our car."

Julie was capable of this overwhelmingly affirmative
manner, but Nicky had never seen it exhibited in just such
a way. The decision having been made, Julie lost no time
with any but the major consideration.

"I should go," Julie said. "I suppose I am responsible, in a
way, for everything. If he had not heard me talking about
Mlengana Rock——"

"That is something I can't understand," said Nicky, "but
I have stopped worrying about it."

They consulted Eric, but Victor Tolley was kept in the
dark. Nicky intended to run away from him and to allow
him to forgive her afterward.

"All right," Eric said, "you two clear out. I've been
wanting to have a go at painting, and this will be my
chance. A fancy struck me that might turn out not so badly
on canvas if I can bring it off. But you, young lady, must
come back in some reasonable time, because I warn you I
can't have Tolley weeping on my shoulder."

Nicky said, "Vic won't do any weeping."

"He might," said Eric. "I wonder if you really know the potentialities of Victor."

The letter from Mr. Hickey said that Nicky must come alone, but this admonition seemed to mean only that the mission and its purpose must be kept a close secret. At all events, she had no car and no other means of getting one, and the joint expedition with Julie seemed to answer every reasonable requirement of the situation. The Germans had left Port Quentin days before, but the air was not yet clear of suspicion. Eric said that he would guarantee to keep things quiet on the home front.

Nicky soon began to have mixed feelings about Julie as a traveling companion. At first she was delightful company, and it was something just to be with a woman so well turned out, so completely the mistress of every situation. But Nicky began to notice how she seemed to classify everything and fit it to her own inflexible system. After all, Julie sometimes seemed less a person than a civilization. Even her small talk was for a purpose—either deliberately to put her companion at ease or to acquire information or to prepare the way for the execution of designs which she was making or had already made. Nicky continued to like and to admire her, but there was a conflict between Julie's good sense, her correct manner, her intellectual purpose and Nicky's own impulsiveness and reliance upon feeling. Nicky did not like to be wholly controlled; she inclined toward action, not toward deliberation.

There was, for instance, the news of the world which

Julie insisted upon getting over the wireless whenever they stopped at any place where this was possible. She made it seem that this journey of theirs was not a personal thing but part of the marching world order, the calamitous progression of events which almost always tired her and made her sad and silent. In one small village, silent in the brilliant sun, they heard that Princess Juliana's baby had been born in Holland—Beatrix Wilhelmina Armgard, Princess of Orange-Nassau—and also that the British steamship *Endymion* had been sunk by a torpedo, with a loss of ten lives, including that of a Swedish non-intervention control officer. But who had sunk the *Endymion* and on what orders no one knew or seemed likely to know.

"Why do I listen to the broadcasts?" Julie asked. "They only annoy and depress me."

But she knew why. It was because she was aware of the dislocations of the European world, and she had a feeling of responsibility which had been bred and educated into her. She had no plan for the conduct of the world, but she had a sense of order which was violated and a distrust in the destiny upon which civilization certainly should have been able to rely. And with this went a desire that someone should do something, although she did not know what. Observing her, Nicky at last thought that she herself was no more at a loss concerning individual problems than Julie was concerning the larger ones.

Nicky began to feel a certain jealousy lest Julie take over completely and conduct the whole affair relating to Hugo; Nicky did not want it that way. She regarded him as her special interest. She did not want to pool him with Julie's world obligations.

That morning when they drove into Lady Elsie Nicky was feeling more rebellious than usual, because Julie was already forming their plans and because the prospect of seeing Hugo was now an immediate possibility. Plans for the more distant future were not so bad, but in the present Nicky wanted only the present itself. She looked about her at the scenery, both at the mountains in the distance and at the countryside bordering the road. Julie was driving, and she looked mostly at the road and at the turns ahead.

Thus it happened that Nicky saw Jacob and recognized him, although he was not wearing the greatcoat but a porter's khaki uniform and a red fez. Julie saw the boy walking along by the road, but she neither recognized him nor gave him a thought.

"Stop!" said Nicky suddenly. "Please stop and let me down, Julie. I want to walk from here. It isn't far."

"Why, child," said Julie, "are you out of your mind?"

"Perhaps," said Nicky, "but you will have to humor me, Julie, really you will."

Julie suspected nothing except a girlish whim; was it some romantic notion or superstition, she wondered? She did not like this sort of thing, because it was a departure from and an interference with intelligent conduct, but Nicky was so earnest that she let her have her way. The car slowed to a halt, and Nicky got out just at the entrance to the village.

"Mind you, come right along now," said Julie. "You really shouldn't be doing anything so silly."

As soon as the car had gone on Nicky turned and walked back to meet Jacob, and the black boy pointed out the place where Hugo was concealed. She did not notice the blood on Jacob's leg.

Now she stood looking at Hugo, and at first she hardly knew him, because his face was so lean and burned, his eyes were so deep, and his uniform was so disguised in dust and caked mud. It flashed into her mind that she had never planned what was to happen when she met him; she had lived over and over many imagined variations of how they might come together, but always at the final moment of reunion and recognition there was nothing definite, nothing but the anticipation and the wonder. She had thought perhaps that she might cry out, "Hugo!" in a small, choked voice and that he might cry out, "Nicky!" and that they might then be clasped together tightly, not needing words. But this did not happen. Hugo looked at her, and she looked at him, and the pause lengthened.

"How did you find me?" he said at last.

"Never mind that now," she said. "How are you, Hugo? Are you all right?"

"I am well enough."

"You look thin and tired."

"There is no need to worry about me. I think I am getting back as I was before that terrible night when I was tricked into deserting my duty."

"Don't look at me like that, Hugo. I did not trick you. I tried to help you."

"How do I know what you did? If it had not been for

you nothing could have made me run off. I am quite sure of that."

"Hugo, I tell you I am with you, not against you. I went to the commandant the next morning and tried to make him believe you were loyal and that you had done nothing wrong. I did, honestly I did."

"That was very kind of you."

"He would not believe me."

"Are you sure you wanted to be believed?"

Hugo was in that state of exaltation to which he had been raised when he struck Jacob. He sneered at Nicky because it was a way of striking her, and the sneer gave him pleasure. This was not because all this while he had been alternating between longing and resentment as she came again and again into his thoughts, although that persisting resentment had something to do with it. This was new, a breaking out of subjection. The whole length and intensity of his ordeal was turning in him, giving sharpness and fervor to his revolt. He felt himself strong and powerful, and he could exact vengeance from those who had wronged him and his country. Deliberately he brought into his mind the thought that Nicky was not really pretty.

"You were not like this," said Nicky. "Don't you remember how you carried me to the beach, Hugo? Don't look that terrible way."

"I remember many things," said Hugo, "but the only thing which is important is the duty I owe to my Führer. I intend to find a way in which this duty can be performed."

"I don't want to stop you. What have I got to do with

your duty? I tell you I have stood up for you. I know I can help you if you will let me."

"I think I had better help myself. I have been very stupid, and I do not intend to be so any more. Because I ran away once I had to keep on running away. I thought I was lost and ruined and that there was no hope for me. Can you imagine anything as stupid as that? Of course there is hope. I am starting out to redeem myself, and it will not be well for anyone who stands in the way."

Nicky had never seen anyone so hard, so cruel and fanatical. She had wanted to cry; she felt that she had been on the verge of hysteria—for this was so different from the meeting of which she had dreamed—but there was a certain touch of realism in her, a clarity of vision, which prevented tears and kept her looking at Hugo stubbornly, wonderingly.

"Hugo," she said, "what are you afraid of?"

"I am not afraid of anything! How dare you say a thing like that!"

"Why should I not dare to say what I think? You are afraid, but perhaps you don't know it."

"That is ridiculous."

"It does seem so, but it is true. How angry that makes you!"

"Yes, and I think you had better go before I do something I shall regret. No doubt there will be somebody to whom you will desire to give word of my whereabouts."

Nicky thought she would not have known him for the same person except for this stiff German way of speaking.

Although he said inexcusable things, he said them in meticulous language; his intemperateness was expressed in diction so tempered that Nicky could almost have laughed. But that was part of the hysteria she was holding back.

"You think I would do that? You think I would betray you?"

"I do not care whether you would or not. I do not know anything about you."

"I thought I knew something about you. That night on the beach it was as if I had known you all my life, but you seem to have forgotten. You have changed so much that I ought to hate you, but I do not."

"No? That is extremely interesting, but I am too busy to concern myself with psychological matters."

"I think I am sorry for you, Hugo."

He had turned away from her with a rude affectation of indifference, and now he turned back so violently that she thought he was going to attack her. Instead of that he controlled himself and then burst into a peal of unpleasant laughter.

"*You* are sorry for *me*," he said coldly. "That is something I am going to be sure to remember."

Nicky stood in silence, and something inside her said suddenly, as if of its own motion, "He does not hate me. There is something the matter with him. He is afraid of something."

She said to him, "I have brought you some cigarettes."

He ignored her, and she tossed the package upon the ground. He knew what she had done, but he did not look.

In a little while he heard other sounds and knew that she had gone.

Julie drove ahead into the village, and, since there was only one hotel, she went directly to the Royal and put her car into the garage, directing a native boy about the baggage, which consisted only of two bags. She walked around the side of the building and into the hotel office by the front door. There was no one in attendance, but a girl in the uniform of a waitress came out of the dining room and greeted her, offering her the register at the desk. Julie registered for herself and Nicky and was shown to a room near the end of the corridor, the black boy following with the bags.

Mr. Hickey was sitting at a table in the dining room with Dr. Weiss, and he had arranged matters so that he might have a view of any arriving guest. His calculation had gone awry, however, since Julie had walked from the garage instead of from the roadway in front of the hotel. He knew that some girl or woman had arrived, and he thought he knew who, although he had not seen her and had not heard her voice clearly.

Mr. Hickey had slept well during the first part of the night but had awaked in considerable perspiration at about three in the morning. His active mind had sought a convenient solution of the problem which he thought should really be no problem at all, since there was no fundamental conflict of interest. Dr. Weiss was welcome to Hugo and to do anything he liked with him, and all Mr. Hickey wanted out of it was a handsome bit of cash. Mr. Hickey was going to get Nicky, too, but that was his own business, and Dr. Weiss was not to stick his nose into that side of the affair. All clear, yet how far from clear!

Dr. Weiss, who was more perceptive and more suspicious than any man should be, had somehow got the idea that Mr. Hickey was playing it double, and Mr. Hickey felt that this idea might turn into something extremely unpleasant and perhaps dangerous. By what stratagems, therefore, could he keep the doctor and Nicky safely apart while the business was concluded? By what show of candor could he convince Dr. Weiss of his single-mindedness in delivering Hugo, yet at the same time prolong the matter enough so that he could win Nicky's confidence and gratitude? Mr. Hickey devoted his best thought to these questions, and it seemed to him that he could get through into the clear, providing he succeeded in collaring Nicky as soon as she arrived in Lady Elsie and filling her with the need for secrecy.

Now that he thought Nicky had shown up at the hotel and gone to her room he acted promptly on an initial bit of ingenuity which the night's planning had suggested. He deliberately spilled his coffee down the front of his suit. He did, however, spill somewhat more than he had intended, and it was hot. He pushed back his chair, leaped up, and dabbed at himself with a napkin.

"What a clumsy biddy I am!" he exclaimed with ruefulness which was partly genuine.

"There is a reason for such things as that," observed Dr. Weiss blandly. "You are excited over something, is it not?"

"It is not," said Mr. Hickey. "You can put that one back in your pocket. I was never less excited in my life."

The waitress, a broad-cheeked girl of Dutch descent, came and began to mop the coffee from the table, but Mr. Hickey said that he was through eating, anyway, and would just go to his room and tidy himself up. He remarked to Dr. Weiss that he would be seeing him again in no time.

As Mr. Hickey went through the office he noticed the last name on the register, and it was Nicky's. She had room 7, and he did not observe that Mrs. Eric Williams also had room 7. He stepped briskly into the corridor, making sure that no one was following or looking after him. Without troubling to knock, he took the knob of the door of room 7 and opened it quickly, stepping inside and closing the door after him. Then he turned and found himself confronting a woman who was a complete stranger. She was looking at him with a keen eye but without any evidence of alarm or, particularly, of surprise. She guessed who he was.

"I'm looking for Nicky Birch," he said.

"She is not here yet."

"I can see that, thank you. Might I ask who you are?"

"I am a friend of Miss Birch. I am Mrs. Williams."

"Didn't she come? What's she up to?"

"She will be here in a little while. She wanted to walk through the town."

"This won't do," said Mr. Hickey. "I told her to come

alone, and I had my reasons. There's danger for you know who."

"Where is he?"

"Who?"

"The German boy."

"I shouldn't be mentioning him if I were you. He's not far from here."

"Have you seen him?"

"Not yet, but I will soon, providing my advice is not disregarded, as in the present instance."

"How do you know where he is?"

"Look here, now, Mrs. Williams, it isn't up to me to answer such a lot of questions. I'm not on the witness stand, you know. My time is limited, on account of another party in this same matter. I make it my business to know things, and Nicky—Miss Birch—has to take my word or else call the whole business off, which I don't believe she will do. The other party I have reference to is a man here who isn't to know that there's anything between me and Nicky or between me and you, which there isn't, so far as I know, and won't be. Do you see? You're please to tell Miss Birch that right away, before she says a word to a soul, and not to forget it yourself. I have to go about a bit with this Dr. Weiss, which is the party's name, for reasons that can wait until later, but the reasons are good ones. It's all in the way of this same business. The thing to remember is that when he's around we don't know each other, see?"

"Very well," said Julie calmly, "although I don't understand the reason for so much mystery. The fact is that I have an interest in the German boy myself, and that is one reason I am here."

"What's that you say?" inquired Mr. Hickey, for Julie's remark fitted exactly into an unfilled place in the puzzle picture as Dr. Weiss had presented it.

"I said I have an interest in the boy. If it had not been for me he would not have levanted——"

"Oh, you're in it that way?" he exclaimed suddenly.

He thought Julie looked as if she might be a secret agent, although she was a lady. She was a cool one, and he did not admire cool women as a rule.

"Anyway," he went on, "you keep it clear what I said about this Dr. Weiss, or all of us will be in the soup, and that's the last thing you want after what you've been up to."

Mr. Hickey started to button his coat and thus unintentionally directed attention to the state of his suit as a result of the spilled coffee. The damage had been conspicuous enough, but there had been no occasion to mention it.

Now he said, "Spilled my coffee down my front like some five-year-old."

"Here, let me help you."

Julie took a clean towel, dipped it in the cold water pitcher, and began sponging Mr. Hickey vigorously. He backed away, and she held him by the coat collar and slowed his retreat. Julie was attractive and in a way perhaps beautiful; there was some faint feminine scent about her, a kind of lavender sweetness, but these allurements Mr. Hickey resisted. The hand which held his coat collar was too firm; the hazel eyes were too much concentrated upon a single object, and instead of trying to kiss her—which would have been his way—he had an unreasonable fear that this competent creature might be scouring his ears next. For the first time since he had achieved manhood he was trying to end instead of to prolong an intimate encounter with an attractive member of the opposite sex.

"You're wetting me through," he told her. "Here, now, let me go, please."

"If you won't stand still I can't do anything. You should have that suit sponged immediately, you know, before the coffee stain is set."

"Thank you kindly," said Mr. Hickey, and made his escape.

It seemed to him that the condition of his clothes, especially with a lot of cold water rubbed on them, did rather cry for attention. He had a look about for the maid and arranged with her to give prompt attention to his job of sponging and pressing. She stood in the hall while he ducked into his room, removed the trousers and coat, and handed them out to her. Then she disappeared in the direction of the kitchen. He believed in traveling light, and he had nothing at all with him which he could put on to make himself presentable, wherefore he sat on the edge of his bed in his underwear and smoked cigarettes, one after another.

Presently he heard footsteps which he hoped were those of the maid but soon made sure were the heavier tread of a man—undoubtedly Dr. Weiss. He did not care to see Dr.

Weiss at the moment, not because of his undressed condition especially, but because he desired a brief respite before being committed to the quest for Hugo Becker or, as he thought of the fugitive, Dr. Weiss's Mr. Smith. He decided against locking the door, which might have been suspicious, and adopted the simpler course of dropping to the floor and rolling under the bed. He was under the bed by the time Dr. Weiss knocked and, the knock being unanswered, opened the door and looked around the room. Mr. Hickey held his breath, but the footsteps did not retreat. Instead, the door closed, and they came on toward the bed, as nearly as he could judge.

"What I want is a bit of quiet," Mr. Hickey said to himself. "Then as soon as I get my trousers back I mean to have a go at Nicky. She has to mind what I say better than she has so far, or I'll know why."

He did not for a moment doubt that his concealment was effectual, and he could hardly believe the evidence of his senses when he was seized by the leg and pulled out upon the floor, in the light of day, with Dr. Weiss standing over him.

"People do not vanish from rooms such as this," Dr. Weiss said severely. "Do you take me for a fool?"

"What's all this now?" complained Mr. Hickey. "Can't a chap have a little privacy?"

He rose from the floor and sat down in a chair against the wall, half plaintive and half alarmed because of the look in the doctor's eye.

"Why do you want to avoid me?" inquired Dr. Weiss.

"Oh, come now, I never had any such idea."

"Do you always hide yourself under the bed when some-one knocks at the door of your room?"

Dr. Weiss pronounced "room" as if it had four "o"s in it instead of two; Mr. Hickey, for the first time, found the German accent distasteful. It seemed too persistent, too in-sinuating.

"I'm not properly dressed," he said. "I was just keeping out of sight a bit until I get my clothes back, that's all."

Dr. Weiss did not sit down, but he walked across to the window and leaned against the sill, looking at Mr. Hickey.

"I am not a fool, if you please," the doctor said stiffly, and Mr. Hickey fancied he could see the moist, open lips and the sinister expression, although, as a matter of fact, he was looking against the light and could see very little of Dr. Weiss's face.

"What is all this mysterious business that you are attend-ing to?" the doctor went on. "I do not trust you, Mr. Hickey. I tell you that quite plainly."

Yet there was no threat. Dr. Weiss seemed to be a matter-of-fact businessman, somewhat tired, stating his position. Mr. Hickey took heart and for a moment con-sidered the truth but quickly decided against it, not on principle, but by instinct.

"The fact is," Mr. Hickey said, "I've been digging up useful information. That's what I've been about, if you must know. I'm in this for business, and don't you forget it. I know it pays for a man in my position to look sharp about him."

"Yes," said Dr. Weiss, "that is true."

"Well!" said Mr. Hickey. "Well!"

"What useful information have you succeeded in 'digging up,' as you say? Just one small piece of information, if you please, Mr. Hickey, for the sake of the confidence which ought to exist between us."

Mr. Hickey's eyes shifted, and he thought fast.

"Anything of value which you convey to me will, of course, be remembered in our accounting at the end."

"Of course," said Mr. Hickey. "Well, here's what I've got hold of just now. This woman in room 7—never saw her in my life before, either, and I can prove that any time you like—she's a British agent. She's the one made your man—I mean, Mr. Smith—take to his heels. Told me so herself, she did."

"So!" said Dr. Weiss.

"Her name is Williams, and she's a kind of a lady, though queer, too, I should say. Well, now, how's that for a bit of information come upon in an odd moment? And how is it for confidence between the two of us?"

"Very well, for the present," said Dr. Weiss. "When you have recovered your coat and trousers I will talk to you again."

He smiled as he left the room, and his glance at Mr. Hickey was almost friendly. Mr. Hickey's own face lighted up.

"Thought he had me!" said Mr. Hickey to himself in a whisper. "But I come out with that just right, and it took with him too. He won't go so fast about suspecting me after this, not when I tell him what he never even dreamed of by himself."

Mr. Hickey lighted another cigarette, and it seemed to him that the future was taking shape in a desirable manner. To play off Dr. Weiss and Julie was certainly a clever stroke, for it would give him greater freedom with Nicky and raise the value of his services to the doctor in the long run. But after another half-hour he began to wonder what could be detaining his clothes. There was no bellpull in the room, and he opened the door a crack and looked both ways in the hall. No maid was in sight, and no one else was in sight either.

"You wouldn't think a maid in a place such as this would forget an important thing like a man's trousers," he said ruefully.

Presently he opened the door again, leaned his head out, and whistled gently. There was no answer of any sort. He closed the door, sat down again, reached for his cigarettes, and found that the last one was gone.

"Damn!" he ejaculated, and then in a voice loud and unrestrained, "Damn!"

15

Almost everything in Lady Elsie seemed to be in miniature, including the hotel. Perhaps this was due largely to
the majesty of the mountains among which the village had
been built and perhaps partly to the pastoral character of
the place. It had not only a doll-house size but a doll-house
simplicity and beauty, free from the stain of an adult and
sophisticated world. The grazing cattle seemed especially
small, because one saw them far away on green slopes,
under the walls of mountains.

The hotel was run by a gentle, round-headed man named
Fitch, who was in his early seventies. He appeared about
the place little, except in early morning and late at night,
and infrequently at mealtimes. The waitress and the chambermaid were his nieces, daughters of a Dutch brother-in-
law, and the guests had most to do with them or with

Tennis and the other black boys for any heavy work or service out of doors. There seemed to be an indeterminate number of black boys.

In addition to the group which was gathering, with purposes so different, because of the affair of Hugo Becker, there was at this time only one other guest, Atlee Hinton, a gentleman farmer whose acres were on the veld on the other side of the mountains. He was looking up some cattle in the neighborhood, either for purchase or for a trade. Hinton was a tall and shaggy man with thick hair, heavy brows, and long, thin cheeks, and he wore a tan tweed coat. When Julie saw him standing on the stoep that morning, with his pipe in his mouth, she was drawn toward him, for she knew his kind, and with little delay she had him engaged in conversation.

Dr. Weiss was in evidence, too, a little distance away, and they talked about him.

"No," said Hinton, "I don't know who he is. I asked him if he was a missionary, and he said no, he was an ethnologist. Likely story!"

"Yet he could be, I suppose," said Julie.

"Yes, of course. Quite. He could be. But it gives me a scrapy feeling to have these unexplained Germans about this way. You know what they're up to in Natal, I suppose? I take the Natal *Mercury,* and they've had quite a lot about it—not about the Germans so particularly, although the Germans are certainly behind the whole thing. It's a non-European front to give solidarity to all the people of color—Zulus, Indians, Chinese, and the rest—against the Europeans. You know what a patchwork Natal is."

"What a fiendish idea!" exclaimed Julie.

"Yes, isn't it? Ironical, too, for the exponents of racism to be up to."

"I suppose there is nothing anyone can do."

"Nothing within the bounds of free government and all that. . . . Did you have any special interest in this man here, this Dr. Weiss, as he calls himself?"

"Only that I was warned against him in a way."

Hinton puffed away at his pipe for a minute or two before he said thoughtfully, "Sometime I should like to deal with this gentry. I fancy I should know exactly how to handle the encounter."

Nicky walked slowly toward the hotel. She did not need to ask her way, for she quickly saw her destination standing near the head of the high street. All the sparkle, of which there had been plenty the past day or two, had gone out of her, and she wondered what had been the use of all her eager interest and of the journey. What had she hoped to accomplish anyway? Had she expected, foolishly, to be able to help Hugo in some way? Or had the whole thing been just her desire to see him again, to know that he was well, and to feel his arms around her? In any case, it was all absurd enough. She wondered what Julie would think, and this brought a grim smile to her lips, because the suggestion of Julie and her intellectualism confronting Hugo as he was now seemed ludicrous. Nicky felt an increasing bitterness which she must have been holding off, uncon-

sciously but nevertheless deliberately. Was it not true that
she now hated Hugo and despised him? She thought that
perhaps it was true.

When she reached the hotel Julie saw that something
had happened, and they went into their room and shut the
door. Nicky told everything, just as it had happened. Julie
made no comment on the fact that Nicky had deceived and
evaded her, for there was much that was more interesting
and important than this, and Nicky had never seemed
more like a child. It was impossible not to be sorry for her.
But what of Hugo? How could one feel about him?

"I wonder," Julie said to herself, "I wonder if I could
talk to him and make him see reason. . . . There was that
time before at Port Quentin . . . I reached him then. . . ."

"I don't think you could," said Nicky. "He's not open to
reason. And, anyway, he wants to be like that."

"A perfect Nazi," said Julie. "He reverted to type because that is what he's been made all these years. What a
grim joke on me! I suppose I wanted to be sure of my
handiwork—since it was I who set him off—and it turns out
that there isn't any handiwork except Hitler's. There isn't
even any of God's."

Against this Nicky found herself protesting, although
she had no wish to argue with Julie. There was no use in
doing so, because Julie always invoked knowledge and
reason far beyond her own range of powers.

"I don't think it's like that," she said. "I don't think Hugo
has really had a chance."

"He's been free, child. Don't you realize that? What can

you say of a human being who has tasted freedom and turns voluntarily back to slavery? That's the chance he's had, and I don't know that anyone has or deserves a better."

"He's been hiding out," said Nicky. "He hasn't had enough to eat, I know. He's been practically alone in a country foreign to him. . . ."

"Yes, but he's been his own master. He's been able to use his own mind."

"I wonder if he has," said Nicky forlornly.

"It can't be that anyone needs conversion to freedom," Julie went on, walking about the room as she talked. "No! One is capable of it or one is not. This boy evidently is not."

"Perhaps you have to get used to being free," Nicky ventured.

"You're defending him in spite of the way he talked to you. I suppose you are still in love with him."

"I don't know," said Nicky. "I think I'll soon be hating him enough. More than enough."

"Why don't you go back and be pleasant to Victor Tolley? Isn't he more your kind, Nicky?"

"I don't know. You think so, don't you?"

"Yes."

Nicky shrugged.

"I must see this German boy myself," said Julie. "I want to know for myself that kind of mind. It will be a lesson." She laughed shortly. "I think when he went away from Port Quentin that night I felt like a creator. I had made a man of a robot simply through the exercise of reason."

"All the time just now I felt as if he was desperately afraid of something," Nicky said.

"Of what? Has he been hunted down so closely?"

"I don't know. I don't think so. I think he felt safe from pursuit. I wonder if he was afraid of being free and of being on his own, now and always?"

"You aren't making things look better for him. Afraid because there is no one to tell him what to do, because he is away from that iron discipline which his Führer imposes upon the mind . . ."

"But, Julie, perhaps it is necessary sometimes to keep on fighting for liberty. . . . Perhaps, anyway, it is necessary for some people."

"But to fight against what? Against shadows?"

"Against oneself perhaps, or in oneself. Is that so strange?"

"It is nothing that I understand," said Julie. "But, at all events, I am going to see him now—as soon as I can. You wait for me here. Tell me how I can find him. I suppose I should be afraid, but I am not in the least."

Nicky told her in detail where Hugo was concealed. But when Julie had made her way to the place of the iron tent near the entrance to town Hugo was not there. The hot sun—and it was scorching hot now—beat down upon little except dust. Dr. Weiss had been before her.

Dr. Weiss had watched Nicky arrive at the hotel on foot, and he had taken note of the absorption with which she and Julie retired to the seclusion of their room. He looked around the premises and considered a number of vantage points from which he might eavesdrop upon what he felt assured would be an interesting conversation. There was the possibility of standing or strolling outside the windows on that side of the hotel, for most of the windows were open; there was the roof which was fairly easy of access and not too steep, and there was certainly the keyhole of the door which opened from room 7 into the corridor. But best of all, he decided, was the adjoining room, which was not occupied.

He introduced himself into this room by the expedient of taking the key from the rack in the unattended office, and by putting his ear against the wall he managed to overhear a great deal which he considered significant. If Mr. Hickey could have witnessed this exploit he would have felt his own market value suffer a sharp decline, but Mr. Hickey was otherwise engaged, or, at least, detained.

Once having learned Hugo's whereabouts, Dr. Weiss waited no longer. He left the hotel, a raincoat over his arm, like any tourist out for a stroll. He seemed unhurried, but he lost no time. Soon he found Hugo, who was alone, and spoke to him in German.

"You are Hugo Becker?"

"Yes. Heil Hitler!" said Hugo, and stood erect, giving the Nazi salute.

Dr. Weiss returned this gesture with an involuntary indication of surprise, not that Hugo should have given the salute—which he might have expected—but because he himself was unused to it, since he had not been in Germany for

many years. He made no immediate explanation of his
presence or his purpose, but Hugo did not question his
authority. His first act was to lead Hugo away from the
camp, so that they might not be interrupted. They sat upon
some rubble at the foot of a steep place where no one could
see them.

Dr. Weiss was not entirely what Mr. Hickey had taken
him to be. He had been, at bottom, a wistful man, but he
had never been original. He had written treatises on ethno-
logical matters in his early days in South Africa which
might as well—or even better, considering the added con-
venience—have been cribbed in any good library at home.
He was so painstakingly thorough that it was not always
apparent to what an extent he relied upon the work of
other and better men, yet none of his writings had attracted
favorable attention, and few had been published until, soon
after the rise of Hitler, he ventured a treatise on the
Volkisch-seelishe Erneuerung, or self-willed regeneration
of a nation, a work of pure inspiration which was praised
by Dr. Goebbels.

Surprisingly, Dr. Weiss was himself aware that he was a
fraud and an imitation, and he was continually playing up
to the conventional, to what he considered the norm. This
made him so trite and tiresome that he was usually bad company, even for himself. When anyone like Mr. Hickey
took him for the real thing he was much pleased and became a bully. As a matter of fact, he had more of the Nazi
qualifications than he credited himself with; his long-
standing frustration passed over easily into cruelty; he

possessed a talent for being regimented, and his emotional
satisfaction in mass movements was unsurpassed. Moreover,
his own realization of being second-rate forced him into the
most devious trickery and cunning.

There was something else about Dr. Weiss, however, and
it showed itself upon this occasion. He was still capable of
being his old wistful self when opportunity offered, as it
seldom did. The difficulty was that he needed to be in the
presence of someone from his own country, almost but not
quite an equal. There had to be a feeling of kinship without
intimacy, of informality without equality, and the necessity
for self-justification had to be absent.

"You have been sent to find me," said Hugo, as if he had
known at once that this was the case and was completely
resigned to whatever might happen.

"Yes, that is so," said Dr. Weiss, looking at the boy with
great interest. Hugo's resignation made it needless to put
on any show. There was no hurry now. "You are younger
in appearance than I thought. You have had a hard time,
have you not?"

"I was not myself, I can assure you. There will be no
more weakness."

"Well, that is a good thing. Once I knew a man named
Becker, at Leipzig, many years ago. He was called Hermann, and he was a fine fellow. I never heard what became
of him. I suppose he could not have been your father."

"No," said Hugo, "my father's name is Ernst. We reside
in Düsseldorf, where he manufactures various instruments,
such as gauges and meters."

"So. I have lost touch with all my old friends, and no wonder! I was an ethnologist, and I came here to Africa when I was much younger. I was interned all through the war, which was very foolish. If we had more leisure I should like you to tell me about Germany and what it is like there nowadays. All that comes to me is terse and official, and one is naturally not expected to ask questions. It is all so changed since my time."

"Germany is now a country of faith and courage——" Hugo began.

"Yes, I have heard that," Dr. Weiss interrupted him quickly. "But what is it really like, I ask? What would it be like to me if I were to go back tomorrow? That is what I cannot imagine—but let it pass. Do not try to tell me. I see that you are like all the others, and I suppose these matters are as they should be. See, I have been giving myself the privilege of talking informally with a fellow countryman just out from home. You think it is odd. Very well, we will get down to business."

Hugo had thought it extremely odd. He had been on the point of despising Dr. Weiss for weakness and inefficiency. The man had been sitting there as if stage-struck, a gentle smile in his mild eyes. But now he straightened, and all expression disappeared from his face.

"As to your own case I can say little. I do not know what will be done. I have my instructions, and I shall disclose them to you as occasion arises. You understand that it is necessary to take strong action under the new regime, for the sake of Germany?"

For a moment Dr. Weiss looked benignant, but he went on quickly, "One thing is important. This whole affair has been most cleverly contrived, more cleverly than perhaps you know, and at the bottom of it is a woman, a British agent——"

"But Nicky—she wouldn't——"

This was still the hard new Hugo speaking, the redeemed Hugo. It would have hurt his self-esteem if Nicky had turned out to be an *agent provocateur*.

"No, you are right. It is not the one you call Nicky. A woman named Williams—Mrs. Eric Williams. You know her?"

"Yes! I detest her."

"Did you know that she contrived everything?"

"No. I still do not see how. But I believe you."

"She is here now, at the hotel in the village. We must trap her, I think, and see if she will talk. I have been thinking that is the thing to do. It will be accomplished best through the young girl, your friend Nicky. It was a mistake, the way you talked to her this morning."

"You know about that?"

"Naturally I know. I am getting to be an old fellow, and I was only an indifferent ethnologist, much as it sorrows me to say so. But for this new work I have a talent. I have been told so by my superiors. What you must do now is to pretend to make love to this girl. You must win her confidence, which will not be too hard, and through her we will get hold of the other woman. You understand? You are quite willing to do this?"

"Nicky won't come near me again."

"You will go to her and draw her aside, out in back of the hotel where there is a secluded place and where no one will be watching except myself. It is quite feasible."

"But how can I go there? Look at me! I cannot be seen like this."

"You will put on this raincoat of mine. I do not think it will rain, after all, and if it does I do not mind being wet. You will go by the side street, but even if you are seen it will make no great difference. Watch your time to attract the girl's attention. Now I will tell you about the arrangements at the hotel and just where you are to go. I will also give you a signal when the time is right. Well?"

"I will do it."

"That is excellent. A little later, of course, there will be a death—after we are through with this Mrs. Williams. That does not surprise you? This is a kind of war we are in, you see. It is what I tell myself. There will be this death, and someone will have to be blamed for it, of course. Do you know who I think will be blamed? This native boy who is with you. Is not that feasible?"

"Jacob! But he would deny that he killed anyone."

"He cannot deny anything when he is dead," observed Dr. Weiss. "He will be blamed only after he is dead himself. That is my idea, and I want to know what you think of it."

"I think it is good," said Hugo.

"Now I must ask this. Have you told the Williams woman anything? Has she obtained information from you?"

"No."

"You are certain."

"Absolutely certain."

"How bungling of her! Yet it might have worked, you know. They might have got you on their side and made you an agent against us, not only here but elsewhere."

"Never!" said Hugo.

"It is well for you to say that," said Dr. Weiss. "I will include your statement in my report. And now please listen carefully, for you are to carry out my orders exactly." He went on at some length, elaborating the plan he had already indicated. "Be sure the girl trusts you completely. That is fundamental. You may then return to your little camp, and I will find you later and inform you of the next step. This much is clear?"

"Yes."

"Very good," said Dr. Weiss, and then he added more slowly, in a return to his first wistful manner, "But one thing I could have wished. If only you could have told me what it is really like now . . . at home. This Hermann Becker I used to know in Leipzig—he was a great drinker of beer. We had good times together, and I should like to meet him again sometime. Well, there is no use dreaming of old times. I don't mind telling you I should be afraid after all these years—like any stranger."

16

Hugo went alone toward the hotel, hatless, and with Dr. Weiss's raincoat covering what was left of his uniform. There were few to notice him along the side streets, and no one seemed particularly curious. As for his own sensations, he was elated because he was about to do something to erase his cowardice and shame and to restore his right to be called a German and a man. This elation burned in him and carried him along. His work had been given him to do, and he no longer had to wonder and to struggle with himself. He was no longer upon his own; he was back in the pattern. He had no doubts, because his instructions were clear, as clear as destiny, and of the same sharp, urgent quality. No, there was not a shadow of doubt in the background of his mind, and the only question, as yet a small one, was whether when the time came for necessary killing he should be the one to do it.

That question, though small, was solemn and not without persistent awe. But he said to himself that if the order should be given to him he would not fail.

"I can do it," he said. "Yes!"

He approached the hotel from the rear and took up his position as he had been told to do. It seemed to him that he waited a long time, and he was impatient because he was being kept from the execution of an important duty. At length Dr. Weiss appeared, at some distance, walking away from the hotel toward the fringe of trees on the higher ground. This was the signal. Hugo tossed a pebble at the window of what he had been told was Nicky's room. A minute later she was looking out, and he was beckoning to her. The plan worked well, step by step; everything had been foreseen, to the smallest detail, for Dr. Weiss was thorough.

Nicky came to join Hugo, full of surprise and curiosity, and he whispered to her the words which had been supplied to him for the purpose.

"I am in danger. You must come with me a little."

He led her back from the hotel, where they were shielded by the galvanized-iron garage. There was open land there and no street, but anyone up above, where the trees were, could see them and very possibly hear them if they happened to speak loudly and clearly.

"Nicky," Hugo said, "can you ever forgive me?"

She stood looking at him, and tears came into her eyes.

"Hugo! Hugo!"

"I cannot tell you what possessed me, to speak to you as I did. Since that moment I have been unable to rest or to find any peace, and I knew I must come to you, no matter what the risk. Nicky, tell me that you will forgive me."

"Yes," she said, her voice choked. "I forgive you then. But I am glad you have come, because I do not know how long the forgiveness would last. Oh, Hugo, I want to help you! I am not your enemy."

They were standing close together, and he put his arms around her and knew that everything was all right and that he had brought it off as Dr. Weiss had ordered. He experienced a thrill of satisfaction and accomplishment—but her hair was against his cheek, and he could not help remembering that night on the beach at Port Quentin. He felt a trembling which at first he thought was Nicky, but then he knew that it was certainly himself. He was still firm, but he had no pride left. He had no conviction. Suddenly he had no strength, and no firmness either. An old longing was all there was, and he was not an arm of Dr. Weiss or of the Reich; he was no more than himself, facing doubt and dismay.

In that same moment he felt himself pushed back, not gently but strongly, and Nicky's eyes were staring into his. Her voice sounded as he had never heard it and as he had never dreamed it could sound.

"Hugo," she said, "how can you be so vile?"

The light in her eyes was hard, and he saw the hatred and contempt welling into them.

"What do you mean?" he asked. "What has changed you?"

"Did you really think you could fool me and twist me around your finger? Did you think I would be taken in by such sham? Oh, I knew at the first moment, but I did not want to know—I would not let myself believe. I fooled my- self—you did not do it. You could not, because I can see through and through you."

"Nicky, Nicky, what have I done?"

He was remembering all that had gone before, and now that it was too late he seemed to feel what he had lost. That reaction which had carried him to such heights, which had seemed the real restoration of balance and sanity and, most of all, his own security, now was past. He was sinking.

"Yes, what have you done? I wonder if you have the decency to understand!"

"Do not speak so loudly, please. I am afraid of what may happen. I am afraid we will be overheard. I tell you I could not go through with it. I was not going to go through with it. As soon as I had you in my arms everything began to be different. If you had not guessed I would have told you myself. I swear I would have done so."

"Is there any way now that you can make me believe what you say? Do you think there is?"

"I beg of you to stay near me and to speak as if we were friends. I beg of you, because I do not want anything to happen."

"We are being spied upon, I suppose," said Nicky. "That is part of the game. Well, I am not afraid. I can't imagine anything worse than the vileness I have seen in you already."

She stood there, blazing at him, at a loss for words to speak, and it would have been impossible for anyone, even at some little distance, to take them for trysting lovers or for friends.

"I am afraid for you," said Hugo, "not for myself. I will not let you be wronged any more. It is true that we are being spied upon, and you must help me make it seem that everything is all right."

He put his arm about her again, and although she was about to resist she did not do so; and now a watcher from the trees up above would have thought them reconciled. Hugo pressed his lips against hers, but her mouth was hard and unyielding. With her eyes so close he could see her anger and the shame of his own treachery. It was more terrible to know so completely from her than it would have been to know only through his own awakening perception. As he touched her, as she was so close to him he kept remembering the day and the night at Port Quentin until the memory was so poignant that he could hardly bear it.

"I have been wrong. I know I have been wrong," he said.

The fear he knew now was different from all the other fears and brought with it what none of the others did, the reflection of its own very opposite, which was hope. How could he hope? But how could he not hope? He despaired and feared, and he hoped, ready to grasp any chance. He was stung to life, and before this he had been alive only in some strange synthetic sense, by reasoning and formula prepared for him. He said to Nicky, the words wrung from confusion and torment, "I would die for you."

"What childish talk is that?" she asked. "I have never understood you—I can see that now. Julie was right. She said you were the perfect Nazi. That was what was the matter with you this morning. You were up to some kind of suicide on the grand scale, a suicide of the soul. Now you want to die for something else. Is that all you can think of? Tell me, are you a human being or are you not? And if you are, why can't you behave like one for a change?"

Hugo did not understand what she meant, and for the moment he could not answer. She was so close, yet she was far away.

"People are supposed to be people, not puppets or dummies," said Nicky angrily. "Are you afraid of life? Are you afraid to be yourself?"

Hugo looked at her as she stood so filled with fire and with passion. She was beautiful to him, but, for all that they were so near, so close that he could have leaned forward and kissed her lips again, it seemed impossible for him to communicate anything to her. He looked at her with a desperate longing for some understanding he had missed, and now he knew that this was the redemption he was after, not the other. This was the only redemption in the world, this girl and what she stood for. He tried, with dry lips, to answer her questions, knowing that he could not.

"I don't know," he said. "There are things a man must do. . . . It was intended that I should serve my country. . . ."

"I would have defended you for that," said Nicky. "I did defend you. But what you tried to do to me just now, to lie, to pretend—— You were going to use me, that's what you were going to do. As if any girl can be fooled by play-acting love! Can you tell me what that was for?"

"That friend of yours, that Julie Williams, is a British agent," Hugo said.

"How perfectly ridiculous! It's not true."

"I am told that it is true. These things have been contrived; they have not just happened."

"You talk like Julie, and I can't argue with you. You make life so complicated and won't believe in the simple things. You must have it sophisticated, and half the time it's not. Of course things just happen, and there's no need to make so much of them."

Hugo looked at her, not knowing what to believe. He wondered if he had ever believed Julie was a secret agent—now it seemed such a made-up story.

Nicky went on, "Julie says you are not capable of freedom or of being your own master."

"What did you say?" asked Hugo.

"Oh, I still believed in you then. I said sometimes a person had to keep on fighting to be free, even when he seemed to be free already. It was probably nonsense. It was just something that came to me."

"But fighting what, how?"

"Yourself, I suppose, in your own head, in your own mind."

Hugo could understand that, because he knew the struggle he had been through, knew it as nobody else could —but evidently he had never known all that it was for, and he did not know now. He was going to say something more, but Nicky cut him short impatiently.

"How long do we have to go on this way?" she demanded. "Has this been long enough to satisfy your Führer?"

They turned and walked along by the side of the garage, his arm around her shoulders, in the attitude of lovers.

"Nicky," he said, "do you hate me?"

"Yes," she said, nothing in her voice but deep conviction.

When they had turned the corner Hugo dropped his arm, and the next thing Nicky knew, he was gone. She had watched him go, but he had walked swiftly, and now that he was out of sight she felt somehow surprised, as if she had expected an end, a conclusion, and there had been none. Slowly she went back into the hotel, knowing that nothing so hateful had ever happened to her before.

Mr. Hickey's involuntary confinement had continued far into the morning before he succeeded in attracting the attention of the chambermaid. Occasionally he opened the door of his room a little, so that he could lean out and whistle. When the maid finally heard him he was shrill with indignation.

"How about my suit?" he yelled. "I call this a bloody imposition."

"Your suit!" said the maid. "It was cleaned up at once, sir, and I thought you had it long ago, I really did. Never you mind, I'll go at once and see where it is."

"You do that, and get a hustle on," said Mr. Hickey, "because I've had enough of this."

His shirt had dried, and he had put it on and knotted his tie. But the suit did not come, for in some strange manner it had disappeared, as no suit had ever done before in the village of Lady Elsie. The best the maid could do was to return with profuse apologies and a serge suit belonging to Mr. Fitch, the proprietor, which was half again too big around the middle. Mr. Hickey put it on, sputtering as he did so, because of the indignity, the breach of his rights, and the state of his temper.

When he went forth in this costume the first person he met was Dr. Weiss, who by this time had already talked with Hugo and was concentrating upon his further arrangements. Since Mr. Hickey now played no part in these plans and since he was under great suspicion of double-dealing, Dr. Weiss did not look upon the man with friendship or patience.

"Have you found anything out? Have you put your hands on anybody?" Mr. Hickey inquired.

"I do not want to be annoyed by you. I do not trust you," said Dr. Weiss severely.

"You haven't found out anything about me," said Mr. Hickey. "I've been square with you, that I have been."

But there was a tone of uncertainty about him, and Dr. Weiss glared at him and asked quickly, "Have you?"

"Yes, and I ask you to remember our bargain."

"I will remember it, but let me remind you of something too. It is not safe for you to try to deceive me or disobey my orders. Look!" The doctor drew from his pocket a small automatic pistol. "I have used this before, and I am prepared to use it again. I will not have my plans interfered with."

"Of course not," said Mr. Hickey. "I'm with you in this business, aren't I?"

"I will not have you discussing it with anyone," said Dr. Weiss. "You are not to speak of this Mr. Smith, by that name or any other, do you understand? You are not to admit that you know of his existence."

"All right, all right," said Mr. Hickey.

Dr. Weiss went on to develop his arrangements, and Mr. Hickey walked wonderingly down the street, at random. He thought that the doctor must be up to something new but doubted that he could have found the German boy so soon. That being the case, the thing for Mr. Hickey to do was to press the search on his own account. This was even more important at the moment than seeing Nicky, which would follow later. Mr. Hickey felt that the whole situation had been badly dislocated during his confinement and he must hasten to retrieve it.

The way to discover the whereabouts of the German boy was to get on the trail of the native named Jacob, the one with the big coat who knew the Nazi salute and called at hotel kitchens. Mr. Hickey kept his eyes open but saw nothing of any importance. He reflected that he was rather estopped by Dr. Weiss's threats and orders from inquiring around the premises of the Royal, but doubtless the doctor was doing that himself. The course for Mr. Hickey, therefore, was to short-circuit the obvious line by making contact somewhere else. He hoped his shrewdness would not fail him, and he started to explore the possibilities of the town.

Before long he met Julie, who was tired and puzzled. She had followed Nicky's directions exactly, but she had not found Hugo, and she did not understand why. She had waited a considerable time at what she thought must be the proper place, but finally it had seemed ridiculous to wait any longer. When she saw Mr. Hickey she determined to see if she could find out something from him.

"Have you seen young Becker yet?" she asked.

"Never heard of him," said Mr. Hickey shortly.

Julie thought at first he was being impudent, and then she was surprised to see that he was plainly frightened. This was something he could not conceal, for he looked around nervously and was edging away to terminate the conversation.

"You know very well," she said. "We were talking about him this morning."

"Not I," said Mr. Hickey. "I never was. I don't know anything about anybody."

Julie could get nothing out of him. She could not get beyond that lurking, stubborn fear, nor would he allow her to bring it any more into the open. She left him, exasperated, and now she had the same upsetting awareness which

was so common in Lady Elsie that morning, that mysterious things were happening, that threats were in the air. This
offended her orderly mind, because there was no reasonable
basis she could find, but, just the same, it was real, and she
was greatly stirred.

She could not find Nicky at the hotel, and finally she
joined Atlee Hinton for lunch. She was glad of his company, for he steadied her nerves, and she could talk openly
with him. But she did not discuss the case of Hugo Becker.
They were through lunch and taking their coffee when Dr.
Weiss appeared and seated himself at his table. He had acquired a newspaper, a copy of the Johannesburg *Star*, and
he proceeded to read it with some absorption as he ate.

"I know this is absurd," Julie said to Hinton, "but I
could be afraid of that man."

"I don't like his kind," said Hinton. "You think he is up
to something here?"

"I know he is."

"It would be satisfying to know exactly what. Perhaps I
could help."

"What little I know I'm not free to tell, not just now. It
isn't enough anyway."

Dr. Weiss made a brief meal, and they were sitting outside, Julie with a cigarette, Hinton with his pipe, when he
appeared. He approached them and put down his newspaper before them, a courteous gesture.

"Perhaps you would like this paper," he said. "It is quite
a recent one, and I have finished with it."

"Thanks," said Hinton.

The newspaper was folded, and as Julie's eyes fell upon it the first thing she saw was a headline over a story which reported the sailing of the *Schleswig-Holstein* from Capetown on her homeward cruise. The warship had gone to keep her further appointments. Julie looked up quickly and saw Dr. Weiss watching her and smiling. She flushed, for she knew that she had betrayed something.

Julie finally found Nicky in their bedroom. The shade was drawn, and Nicky was lying on the bed in the darkened room, crying. But there was nothing she could tell Julie, nothing, and Julie sat there, silent and puzzled, trying to exercise her processes of reason.

Hugo Becker did not go back to the improvised camp near the entrance to town for many hours. He did not know just where he did go, for he had no purpose except to be alone.

"Am I a human being or am I not?" he asked himself, muttering with his lips. "What am I like? What should I do now?"

But, in the long run, there was little order in the tumult which was in progress in his mind; he was filled with rambling memories, with snatches of self-justification, with reasoning which lacked the proper steps and connections, with shame for what he had tried to do to Nicky. Shame was strong. It could hardly have been stronger. He began to be ashamed of many things, even of having struck Jacob, because he remembered now that Jacob had traded the pistol for the meat which he had been ordered to bring—not simply for his new raiment—and Hugo had eaten of the meat most eagerly. He was ashamed of the whole attitude he had taken, because it was an attitude he could not possibly have sustained. He was not bold and reckless. He was not cruel. He was soft and gentle. He wished that he might be a child again and have things natural and comfortable about him—but this was not in words but in memories which came in small fragments to pull at him and to comfort him in turn. He was ashamed of being so soft too.

"O God," he said, "what am I? What am I to do?"

At last he went back to the camp, hoping that Dr. Weiss would not come. He waited impatiently for Jacob, and Jacob was late because he had a bundle to bring in secret from the prying eyes of the village. Jacob had Mr. Hickey's checked suit, cleaned of coffee and newly pressed, wrapped in brown paper which he had managed to acquire through his back-door connections at the Royal Hotel.

Quickly Hugo changed into Mr. Hickey's clothes which fitted him indifferently and told Jacob to burn the uniform without loss of time. He did not care if the smoke from the fire was seen. Jacob gathered a little kindling, and the blue cloth burned with a strong smell. But Jacob could not allow the gold-threaded swastika on the coat sleeve to burn; when Hugo was not looking he tore the swastika away and put it in the pocket of his khaki tunic, along with the other bright objects he was treasuring.

"We are going away," Hugo said. "We must go swiftly, and we must not be followed."

"Yes, baas," said Jacob.

They got together their possessions which were worth taking, and soon they were on their way, leaving Lady Elsie behind them as rapidly as they could make their feet move over the ground. This was not like the first flight, which had been a strange, unconsidered thing; this was a fleeing which was in earnest, prompted by instinct and by reason alike. Hugo was running away from Dr. Weiss and the doctor's plans, from what they represented, but he was going toward something as well; despite the great burden which he carried, he felt within him for the first time on this continent the stirring of a forgotten spirit of adventure. Hope was what made that possible, hope and the fact that he had begun to learn something about himself as a single, separate person with a place not yet found in the world.

One thing, however, had not changed since that other venture into the unknown: a longing for Nicky would not die or be hidden or denied. It would not stay out of his mind.

Dr. Weiss had looked for Hugo at the camp in vain several times, and when he went to the place in the evening he was surprised to see the embers burning out where Jacob had made the fire. He sat on the ground and smoked a cigarette, for he did not doubt that Hugo would return before long. Everything was going so well that the doctor permitted himself to feel sentimental and his thoughts to wander. He thought of his youth in Leipzig and some of the questions he might ask young Becker.

But presently it began to seem to him that there was

something surprising about that remnant of coals and ashes. Why had the fire been made, and, since it had been made, what was the reason for Hugo's continued absence? The ash had a queer look. Dr. Weiss poked about with a stick and soon he found buttons which were easily recognized. Hugo's uniform, then, had been burned. That meant, first, that Hugo had obtained something else to wear and, second, that Hugo had—yes, that was certainly it—gone away. The doctor looked all around the camp, at various odds and ends strewn here and there, as it now seemed, in haste.

"I have been betrayed!" he exclaimed. "He has fooled me."

As he had often said, Dr. Weiss believed that matters such as this did not just happen but that they were contrived, cunningly contrived. He applied his powers of analysis, and it seemed to him that he could reconstruct what had occurred. The man Hickey was certainly involved. Dr. Weiss admitted regretfully that he had underestimated Hickey sadly.

"So he was without his coat and trousers," the doctor mused, "for the excellent reason that he had arranged to supply them to young Becker. It is a reasonable assumption. I do not even doubt now that Hickey knew about his running away and may have helped plan it. That was the reason for his peculiar behavior."

Dr. Weiss paced up and down excitedly. He could not understand how he had been so mistaken in young Becker. He had liked the boy. He would have sworn that Becker would have obeyed orders implicitly. It must have been the girl who had changed him. She had been conveying messages to him all the time they had pretended to be innocently making up a quarrel. Dr. Weiss was outraged and bitterly resentful at the manner in which he had been fooled all day, and he did not doubt they were all laughing at him.

His plan was ruined, his beautiful plan which he had developed with such finesse, every contingency provided for. But Dr. Weiss knew what he was going to do.

Julie and Nicky sat on the stoep at the Royal Hotel with Atlee Hinton, sipping their sundowners. The air was cooler, and the mountains were changing color, and the miniature town was about to be absorbed into a peaceful and sleepy dusk.

They talked of the native problem and of the coming election. Hinton said he thought the Union party would certainly hold its own and perhaps gain considerably. He expressed the sharpest disapproval of Dr. Malan. After a little while Mr. Hickey came along, returning from his explorations. As he approached they saw that he was in a fine state of cheer, evidently having treated himself well. Julie was puzzled, because when she had last seen him he had been frightened, and now he was half drunk and strutting like a tomcat.

"Have you seen Dr. Weiss?" he asked them. "He wants to see me, though he don't know it, and I want to see him. You know the gentleman I mean?"

This speech was somewhat blurred, and as he delivered it Mr. Hickey looked at them with a leer which said as plainly as he could have put it in words, "I know something. I've got hold of information which puts me on top after all." This was quite true, for Mr. Hickey's afternoon labor had not been in vain; he, and he alone, had seen Hugo and Jacob start on their flight, and he alone knew how they could be overtaken.

"We haven't seen Dr. Weiss," said Atlee Hinton shortly.

Mr. Hickey shambled past them into the hotel, and they could hear him opening and shutting doors. Nicky realized that she had never spoken with him and thanked him for his help. She almost went to overtake him, and then thought better of it, and by this narrow margin lost the opportunity to acquire information which, in his condition, he might have communicated to her gladly. In a few minutes he came out again and walked down the steps past them.

"I'll find the old boy," he said with a wink. "He'll be glad to see me."

"Unpleasant character, that," remarked Hinton.

"He can be kind," said Nicky.

"I wonder what he wants Dr. Weiss for," said Julie. "Do you suppose he has something to tell him . . . ?"

To Julie the whole day had been largely a mystery, for she had not succeeded in finding Hugo and she had no explanation whatever for Nicky's strange behavior, for Dr. Weiss's place in the progression of events, or for Mr. Hickey's rise from the depths to the heights. She made up her mind to have a few words with Mr. Hickey before she went to bed that night. Mr. Hinton was talking on in his deep, pleasant voice, but she began to miss the sense of what he was saying; she began to brood upon the violated order of her world.

It was long after ten o'clock when she found Mr. Hickey, in his room, but she had no words with him whatever, for Mr. Hickey was quite dead. He had been shot, several times, and he lay on the bed as if he had been thrown there. But Julie thought as she stared in surprised horror that there was still upon his face a reflection of that final leer of triumph, that confidence in his own superior position in this whole affair. There was also perhaps a beginning of the astonishment he must have felt when his lips were sealed forever upon the information of which, as he well knew, Dr. Weiss stood in special need. Mr. Hickey in life had always appreciated irony, but this was beyond him.

Then Julie, the cool, the controlled, the intellectual, uttered a scream which sounded loud through the little hotel and brought all the others running.

17

THE POLICE seemed to think robbery was the motive. They made a great deal of the disappearance of Mr. Hickey's suit and questioned the hotel people closely about it, but they would have made much more if they had known about Hugo Becker. There was no one to inform them concerning him. Julie would have told, but some characteristic inhibition held her tongue; she felt that this was an episode in a larger, still mysterious international intrigue toward the solution of which the ordinary police could be of no help. In response to questions she would have answered frankly, withholding no information, but the questioning did not lead to Hugo.

Dr. Weiss would not have told under any circumstances, for the official version was that no one had deserted from the *Schleswig-Holstein.* It was his cardinal purpose to make the facts correspond with the official version. It must have occurred to him that he could set the police after Hugo, with the strong chance that Hugo would be arrested in the dead man's clothes, a stroke with something to commend it, but this would have spread the story of the desertion far and wide and rendered impractical the future plans which the doctor hoped to mature. He wanted to work through Hugo to enmesh the enemies of the Reich who were in this business.

As for Nicky, she would not have told, either, and she was the only one who felt sorry for Mr. Hickey and would gladly have turned up his murderer. She did not know what to think. She did not believe that Hugo could have killed Hickey, although on most reasonable grounds this was plausible. She did not go by reason. She hated and despised Hugo, but these emotions were not constant; they had intervals of lifting like clouds, and then was when she wondered most. Had he gone away before or after the murder, and if before, why? Had he been stung into flight by the contempt she had heaped upon him? Had he really run away to be free? Julie's failure to find him during the previous afternoon made it appear that he had gone long before evening, and in that case perhaps he could still be saved. But she thought that he would have to save himself now. She could do nothing, and she expected never to see him again.

"Of course," Atlee Hinton said to Julie, "you and I feel certain this Weiss chap had something to do with it, but the police can't find any evidence. I don't mind saying I tried to put them onto him. His story is perfectly straightforward,

and I'm told there's no reason to hold him any more than
there is to hold the rest of us. They can't even be sure just
where Hickey was shot or when. It's not unlikely he was
killed outside somewhere and his body thrown in there to
be found."

"I still have a feeling that Hickey was looking for Dr.
Weiss to tell him something important. . . . Earlier he had
been afraid of Dr. Weiss, terribly afraid. There was no mistaking that. He thought there was some reason why he need
not be afraid any longer."

"Yes," said Hinton, "and in spite of that he just got
liquidated. Why? We don't know. But one thing is sure, I
promise you—that I'm going to take this Nazi business
pretty seriously after this. I've heard about the Germans
down at the Cape, and this non-European-front business in
Natal has made me boil. It won't be healthy for them to try
anything of the kind around my diggings."

Julie was anxious to leave Lady Elsie as soon as possible,
and Nicky, still secretive and repressed, fell in with the
suggestion. They packed their things quickly. But Nicky
said she must go to Durban, as she had promised Hugo at
Port Quentin on the night of the first flight, to meet the
cruise ship *Pretoria* and to find Hugo's parents and tell them
what she could of their son. Nicky had not forgotten, and
she had kept up with the marine news in the papers, so that
she knew the *Pretoria* was due somewhat later than sched-
uled. As it turned out, the *Schleswig-Holstein* had been
gone some days, and if Hugo had been aboard he would
have missed the rendezvous with his parents.

"You shouldn't go," said Julie. "It will do no good at all. Did he have the effrontery to bring that up again after all the other?"

"No," said Nicky. "Perhaps he would not want me to go now, but I promised. Anyway, I'm not thinking of him."

"Are you sure?"

"Yes, of course I'm sure. If he lives or dies it can't be anything to me now, Julie."

"Then you must come back to Port Quentin directly with me. The sooner all this is over and done with the better."

Nicky did not know how to cope with Julie when she was in this mood, for Julie made her feel that all reason and propriety were against her. Until so much had happened Nicky would not have questioned this attitude, but now she felt that Julie was only being domineering and only putting in reasonable and convincing form emotions and desires which were no different in character than Nicky's own.

"I've just remembered something I ought to have told you," Nicky said. "They think you're a British agent."

"Who?"

"The Germans. Hugo said so."

"Why didn't you tell me?"

"I am telling you. I forgot until now. I haven't felt like talking about things."

"But why on earth should they think so? I've done nothing."

"I don't know. It is crazy, isn't it?"

Julie's attitude of reason and calm was shattered. She lighted a cigarette, took a few puffs, and then put it out again.

"I'm sorry," said Nicky. "I thought I ought to tell you. Put you on your guard, you see."

"Of course. But I've never faced anything like this before. It's grotesque. It makes one feel so queer."

"About going to Durban," said Nicky, "I'm afraid I must."

"All right," said Julie, "Durban it is. I don't suppose it. matters."

They started at once in Julie's car, and after a while Julie said, "If I were you I really would forget all about that German boy as soon as possible."

"That's what I'm going to do."

"Victor Tolley cares about you, you know, and he's a good sort. You used to like him, didn't you?"

"I like him now," said Nicky.

As soon as they had gone from the hotel Dr. Weiss made inquiries as to their destination and learned that they had given Durban as a forwarding address. That seemed to him an obvious blind. It was not plausible to believe that Hugo Becker's trail would lead back to the coast, and he had no doubt that they, like himself, would be picking up that trail as quickly as possible. Dr. Weiss shook his head.

"Now," he said to himself, "I must try to think out where they are really going. We will certainly meet again, but I do not believe it will be in Durban."

The sun rose in a limpid sky over Durban to pet and fondle a city grateful for the attention. Instead of being languid in the endless warmth, Durban stirred and was busy about her affairs, which were the affairs of many races and of many different kinds of men. Zulu ricksha pullers, fearfully clad in horns, feathers, and beads, waited in front of the city hall for fares. Retired gentlemen in white played at bowls near the ocean beach. Goods trains went climbing up the steep slopes to the interior, hauled by electric engines. American tourists walked along the esplanade under the palms. The Indian market, sprawling and noisy, milled with merchants and customers, and just across the way the native market milled, too, but with different merchants and different customers, as if it had been a thousand miles apart.

Across the harbor at the bluff lay the British freighter *Silverpine* while the chutes sent manganese ore roaring down into her holds, ton after ton, which she was presently to take to Germany. The English captain did not think much of this, and his pretty young wife thought less. And at a berth along the point docks the German cruise ship *Pretoria* shone in the sun, dapper and sleek, the very pattern of a modern luxury liner.

Nicky had met Mr. and Mrs. Ernst Becker and Hugo's younger brother Otto, who seemed to be about ten years old. Mr. Becker was a large, good-natured man, with hair cut rather short and standing up at the forehead. He had a heavy face, but it was not sluggish, for his smile came and went like the smile of a child, gently, and Nicky saw that he was greatly enjoying his tour. She shrank from the thought of what she had to tell him. He wore a wing collar, and the suit in which he was dressed was obviously his best, not new, but carefully preserved. Mrs. Becker was not so tall as he, but she was large, too, and Nicky noticed how her face must once have been much thinner, yet its younger delicacy was not all gone. She was a good *Hausfrau* type, Nicky thought, but to say only that about her would be to conceal rather than to reveal what she was really like, for underneath she was not a type at all, any more than her husband or her sons. She smiled eagerly, and when she looked at Otto it was with fondness.

Otto was slight of build, an almost fragile child, and his face was thin and pale. He wore a cloth cap with a shiny visor made of imitation patent leather, and under the cap his blond hair peeped out in separate locks. But it did not cover the blue veins which showed through the skin of his temples. He said little, but his eyes peered everywhere, and he was always taking his mother by the hand.

"Otto! *Sieh!*" she exclaimed. She was pointing to one of the great red blossoms of a flamboyant tree, most of the others being out of bloom. Otto's eyes opened wide.

They were going to take a ride on the sight-seeing bus— or did one have to call it the *char-a-banc?*—Nicky was going with them if she wished. She said she did wish.

"But how can I tell them?" she asked herself. "They are good people. They deserve to have a good time, and I must spoil it all for them."

Mr. and Mrs. Becker both knew some English, but, whereas he could carry on a conversation fairly well, she spoke with a hopeless accent and kept getting words all mixed up. They knew Nicky was a friend of Hugo's, but they had waited politely for her to make a further explanation in her own good time. They must have been used to patience, Nicky thought.

The driver of the bus was a cheerful young man in a white duster who asked everyone to call him Billy. His face was red and almost always smiling. As the bus drew out from the curb he called over his shoulder, "Everybody happy?"

Most of the seats were taken, and there was a stir of voices and of giggling. Mr. and Mrs. Becker and Otto peered out of the window earnestly, eager to miss nothing. The bus went through busy streets toward the native and Indian markets, and everyone got out to walk through the markets. Billy advised the tourists to buy bananas with which to feed the monkeys later on the tour, and Mr. Becker bought enough to fill a paper bag. He also bought a highly polished horn of some native animal, the end of which had been carved into the image of a bird.

They were off in the bus once more and going along rapidly, because they were out of the center of the city and traffic was not so constant; soon they swung into a wide drive and crossed a bridge over a river. Finally the bus halted at a place where there were heavy trees close together, wonderfully dark green, on both sides. The scenery looked like that of a park, but it was like real country too. Billy went to the edge of the road and began to call out loudly.

"Jocko! Jocko! Jocko!"

At first there was no response, and the people from the bus who had stepped down into the road stood watching curiously, and some anxiously. Billy kept calling. Then the monkeys came, a troop of almost all ages and expressions, emerging from the trees and confronting the tourists who threw the bananas they had bought in the Indian market. Otto squealed with excitement as he tossed his bananas, one by one, into the hands of the ludicrous creatures who were so grotesquely suggestive of human beings. Some of the monkeys were acquisitive, and some seemed easily satisfied. Mr. Becker laughed with pleasure and held Otto protectively by one hand.

Nicky stood close to Mrs. Becker and tried to see with her eyes but then did not want to do that, for it would not do for her to cry. Mrs. Becker seemed a person meant for this sort of thing, for going out with her husband and child to enjoy their enjoyment, to look after them, to provide for them the sustenance of their bodies and much of that of their spirits. She was too simple and uncomplicated to deserve the penalty of suffering from a cause tortured and obscure.

The bananas were all gone, and the monkeys retreated into the woods, chattering, evidently complaining. Their eyes were bold and impudent. Billy herded his passengers back into the bus.

"Everybody happy?" he called, and on they went.

The destination now was a tea garden, high up, where there were small rustic buildings set about under trees, and a view. Everyone got out again, and there was ample time for tea or a walk. Nicky went with the Beckers to a table at one side, and a waitress came and took their order.

"Hugo," asked Mrs. Becker, "he *vas wohl?*"

Then Nicky told them, as simply as she could. Hugo had not sailed with the *Schleswig-Holstein*, and she did not think he could go back to Germany again. He had done nothing wrong—she told them that, although now she herself was not so sure—but there had been a misunderstanding. He could not explain. The only thing for him to do was to get away and stay in South Africa. Nicky did not look at Mrs. Becker then.

"What kind of misunderstanding?" Mr. Becker asked.

"It's hard to tell you," said Nicky, for the whole complicated sequence of events was too much to make clear. "They thought he had turned against Herr Hitler. He had not, but that was what they thought."

"Yes, yes!" said Mr. Becker. "We have known of these things. It has happened so in Germany, but not to us, never before to us. We have been so careful, Fräulein Birch. We have served our country in everything."

Mrs. Becker began talking in German, rapidly but evidently with a jumble of ideas, hopes, suggestions. Nicky could not understand her. She was crying only a little. Otto sat there not saying a word, looking frightened. Then Nicky had to go through the whole story from the beginning while Mr. Becker's eyes stared at her and did not leave her for a minute. At the end he could hardly have understood much more than he had seen at the beginning.

"It has happened so, but not to us, never before to us"—
that was what he understood. The precise point, the evil
chance which had turned the scales was beyond him, just
as it was beyond Nicky herself. But he seemed to be able
to take it for granted.

"I tried to tell the commanding officer," Nicky said. "He
did not even want to believe me. It was so unfair!"

"A man who worked in my office for many years," said
Mr. Becker, "there was something reported about him. I
do not know what it was. They took him away, and no
explanation was made. I could not ask. Yes, that is the way
it happens. There is no help for it, Fräulein, but that it
should happen to us! I tell you we have been so careful,
and in all things we have given our full duty to the new
Germany."

He sat there, fingering a menu but making no other motion, and the sadness was all the greater to Nicky because
she saw in his eyes the terrible acceptance of this fact, this
unrighteous fact, which should have touched off anger and
indignation. But in this they were far apart, without common ground, and she began to understand that also and to
pity the lives bound so narrowly in set channels, without
the possibility of escape.

Mrs. Becker spoke again in German, and her husband
said to Nicky, "She thinks maybe I could see Mueller at
home. But what would be the use? Who is Mueller? He
could do nothing!"

"Hugo iss gut boy," said Mrs. Becker, trying to smile.

"Of course he is," said Nicky.

"He is still young," said Mr. Becker. "It is not so easy for the young to be careful. When I was his age I was very, very foolish, but it did not matter then."

Mrs. Becker burst into volubility, and she and her husband talked together rapidly in their own language with earnest and guttural expressiveness and with gestures.

After a little Mr. Becker turned to Nicky and said, "My wife wants me to tell you what a good son Hugo has been. When he was a little boy he was very much like his uncle, her brother, who became a minister. We thought maybe he would be a minister of the church also, for he was always reading serious books and would have such a sober face even when his friends were laughing. He won a fine prize in the gymnasium. My wife has it at home now, in Düsseldorf. It is a book cover made from leather and silver. We were proud when Hugo brought home that prize, Fräulein Birch.

"Sometimes we would go on picnics in those old times, and Hugo knew all the names of trees and plants, for he was much interested in those things. Yes, he was a studious child always but good at most kinds of outdoor sport also. When he decided he would go into training for the navy they were very glad to have him. Yes!"

"Was there a girl with yellow pigtails?" asked Nicky.

"*Ja, ja!* Elsa, or maybe Bertha also—but who told you about yellow pigtails? That was a long time ago."

Nicky said to herself, "I can't stand this. Hugo, Hugo, why are you not here? Why are you not here as you used to be? I cannot do anything for you any more. I want to

escape. I don't want to know anything more about you."
Mr. Becker smiled, thinking of that long time past, but
he had no smile for the present.

"It must be time for the bus to start again," Nicky said.

"We see so many changes in Germany, Fräulein," Mr.
Becker went on in a different voice. "Only since we came
here have I heard that the Führer is now chief of the national defense. Von Blomberg and Von Fritsch, those two
are gone, and it is a very great change, I can tell you. If only
we could have this new Germany without such troubles for
some innocent people! Nobody ever knows what is coming
tomorrow. But everything will come well in the end, and
you must not have a wrong opinion of us. What is done
now, though it may hurt, is necessary to be done, it is very
certain."

Mrs. Becker wiped her eyes with a handkerchief and
said something more which her husband interpreted for
her: "We think maybe it is better Hugo had his trouble
here than at home if it had to happen. He will be safe, do
you think? He has friends?"

"I am his friend," said Nicky, but she had not meant to
say that, and she felt she was not telling the truth.

And now the bus was ready to start, and the passengers
were being called. Mr. Becker picked up the polished horn
with the carved bird, and Mrs. Becker took Otto by the
hand. Three of them now, Nicky thought, with the hesi-
tant pleasure of their sight-seeing and their tour crushed
about them. In what plain clothes, in what gentle and obscure souls tragedy chooses to walk—and because the clothes

are plain and the people humble and hidden like pebbles on the beach or leaves in the forest no one considers that the tragedy is really great; this, too, Nicky thought. Mr. Becker helped his wife into the bus. Some girls already seated were giggling.

Billy, the driver, called out over his shoulder, "Everybody happy?" And the bus started back again toward the heart of Durban.

Mr. Becker spoke to Otto in German, smiling as he did so, quite gaily—but not with his eyes, which were distant and sober—and Nicky knew he was saying something like this: "Were not those monkeys amusing? You will have a great time telling your friends about those monkeys, my son."

18

Getting back to Port Quentin was, after all, quite like getting home. Julie drove up in front of the familiar door of the Beach Court, and she and Nicky got out into the dust and looked about. No one came, and they entered the bare, deserted office. It did not seem to be a place where anything remarkable could ever have happened. There was nothing for them to do but to carry their own bags or allow them to remain for the time being under the balcony.

"Vic! Oh, Vic!" called Nicky, but there was no answer. She said to Julie, "Well, after all, I am the hostess here, unless Vic has discharged me, and I welcome you to the Beach Court Hotel. Tea will be ready in a little while."

"Thank you, my dear," said Julie. "I could do with a spot of tea."

Nicky turned toward the bar, feeling sure that Victor

would be there if anywhere. Surprisingly, he was not to be found, but Eric was standing behind the counter in the private bar, with an apron tied around his middle. He was smoking his briar, and there was an air of contentment about him which seemed almost scandalous.

"What are you doing?" inquired Julie, who had followed in Nicky's footsteps.

"Hello, old girl," said Eric. "Well, I'm carrying on for Tolley a bit, you see. He's appointed himself a search party of one to go looking for Miss Birch, and he had to have someone who would defend the home front."

"Eric!" Julie exclaimed. "You mean you haven't told him yet where we went and what for? You haven't told him Nicky was with me?"

"I planned to after a safe interval," said Eric, "but it turned out there was no safe interval. There would have been no holding the man down. I shouldn't be surprised if all of us had failed to recognize in Mr. Tolley the makings of an excellent bloodhound."

"Do take that apron off and come out!" Julie told him.

"Always thought I should have been rather good at keeping a pub," said Eric.

"Poor Victor!" Nicky said. "I've treated him badly."

"That you certainly have," observed Eric, "but it's given him quite a lift in a way. I never saw a chap sharpen up so."

Eric went for their luggage, and they repaired to the balcony as soon as possible to tell him what had happened during their trip of adventure. Julie was cross because they had to wait for tea. Eric leaned against the rail, smoking and looking at them as they spoke, and they settled back in the old chairs. Julie dropped her traveling manner and put her feet on the railing as she had done on the morning when Nicky had first talked with her and admired her. But there was nothing in the long recital which led to any conclusion. After the first, Nicky left the talking to Julie and stopped listening, even, because the story was not her story. Her own story she did not choose to tell, and she sat looking at Eric and Julie and thinking of them and how her own attitude toward them had altered.

When they went back indoors Julie stopped before a recently painted canvas which stood on a table in the upper passage, between the balcony and the hall. The painting was a landscape in strong colors, showing the mountain above the mouth of the river. It had no draftsmanship whatever. but the color was arresting.

"Do you like it?" Eric asked.

"It's in a new manner for you," said Julie, studying the picture. "I wonder what you were about with those gobs of raw color."

"You don't like it?"

"Oh yes," said Julie. "There's something you make one feel. It's only that I can't help being surprised. You've never gone off on that line before. You've always scoffed at the extreme-modernist business."

"Good!" said Eric. "Better tell Tolley you like it. He'll be pleased."

"Why?"

"It's his. It's not mine. I persuaded him to take my paints

the other morning, to get his mind off his troubles, and this
is what he did with them."

Eric stood in front of the canvas, his hands in his pockets,
swaying back and forth with a satisfied smile.

"You swine!" Julie said to him. "You made me think it
was yours."

"I didn't make you think so. You jumped to the conclusion. Now I suppose you'll say you don't like it, after all."

"Of course I don't. It's a daub." Eric laughed as she said
this. "Don't laugh that way. You know I hate being taken
in."

"So do I," Eric said.

"I want to see what you've done yourself."

"I'm afraid I can't put my hand on either of them. You
see, there've been only two."

"You've destroyed them?"

"Yes," said Eric. "You see, they weren't good. You would
have said you liked them, just to encourage me, but you
would really have thought them pretty awful."

Julie and Eric went along the hall to their room, both
aroused, both a little angry, and Nicky descended the stairs
slowly and thoughtfully. It was not long ago that she had
seen them for the first time and placed her faith and admiration in them because they came from far off, representing
all that she thought was pleasant and wise in life. There
had been upon their manner the stamp of something completely civilized and certain. They were, in short, intelligent and sophisticated, traveled and educated, and the cul-

ture and temper of their race sustained them on a plane of
their own.

But now Nicky knew, still wonderingly, that Eric was
an indifferent painter and that Julie lacked real purpose and
direction. Yes, strange as it was and strange as it would
have seemed to Julie herself, she and Eric were only float-
ing. They were in the great drift, like Nicky, like Victor
Tolley, like Hugo Becker and his parents and his small
brother Otto, and all the others.

The thing about life, Nicky had begun to understand,
was living, and there came a point as to that when no per-
ceptions or admonitions except one's own could be of any
help.

Victor Tolley appeared at last, dressed in his usual in-
formal manner but with an overly large pith helmet on his
head. He had left the native boys who had accompanied
him, probably at the rear of the hotel, and he entered alone,
mopping his forehead. He saw Nicky coming from the
lounge to meet him.

"Nicky," he said, "where on earth have you been?"

"I'm sorry, Vic," she told him. "I didn't mean to worry
you."

"This was the worst scare I ever had, and I've been out
almost every day having a look for you. I would have put
the police on, except that Mr. Williams said it would be a
mistake."

"He was to have told you as soon as Julie and I were out
of the way."

Nicky sat on the edge of a chair and began to explain about Mr. Hickey's letter, her strong compulsion to find Hugo Becker and help him, and most of what had happened in Lady Elsie, but not all. He listened without interrupting, but at times he was almost excited and could not refrain from taking a turn about the room, which was the hotel lounge. When she had finished they were both silent for a minute or two.

"Anyway," Victor said, "if you'd been anywhere about here I should have found you. I've hunted in all the likely places and then in the unlikely places."

"But, Vic, I wouldn't just disappear. You should have expected me back."

"Amnesia was my theory," said Victor. "Not at first, but toward the last. Odd things like that do happen, you know —loss of memory and all. I'm not the kind to sit by. I like to be doing something when there's any kind of situation."

"You shouldn't have been neglecting the hotel. How has it been going?"

"Not bad, Nicky, not bad in the least. We had three guests over the last week end, and there've been some inquiries and quite a few bookings. Then of course Mr. and Mrs. Williams are real regulars now. I've got some new plans, too, Nicky. I must tell you about them."

"The outdoor swimming bath?"

"Well, that will come, you'll see. But these are other ideas. When there's more time I'll go into them."

He paused, and she looked at him and felt that she had been unkind and unfair. He was obviously disappointed with the way things had turned out, for he had been kept in the dark and rather made a fool of. He had always been frank and natural with her, ever since their childhood friendship, but now he had not been saying what was really in his mind. He had been talking just to keep up appearances.

"Nicky," he said.

"Yes, Vic."

"Will you walk to the beach?"

"Yes," she said.

It was afternoon now, and although the sun was still warm there was a stir from the sea. The waves sounded along the crescent of sand. They took the shortest way, across the square and through the intervening waste, not the path Hugo and Nicky had followed. Soon the white sand was under their feet, and the brown waves came rolling in toward them, breaking and gathering froth.

Victor took Nicky's hand which was next to him, and she did not draw it away, and when he was sure of that much he said, "Are you in love with that German boy, Nicky?"

"No, I am not," she said, and meant it.

"That's something anyway. He was a fine-looking young chap."

"Yes."

"You liked him, I rather think. You wouldn't have wanted to help him as much as you did or go to such lengths if there hadn't been something. I mean, it wouldn't hold water now, would it, Nicky?"

"Oh, Vic," she said, "I can't talk about it much now. It's all over, really it is, whatever I might have felt or might have thought. Do you know what Julie said about him? She said he was the perfect Nazi. That ought to put you at rest about him, Vic."

"Did she say that? I suppose she had reason. I've missed you all this time, Nicky."

"Perhaps I've missed you. At least it is good to be back where everything is safe and solid, where you feel you belong, as you do at home."

"That's very nice," Vic said, brightening. "I've wondered all along where you might be, and I began thinking what if you'd lost your memory for a bit and were knocking about some of these small places where nobody might say a word or keep an eye out. That Eric Williams, he was no help."

"He should have told you, but he was only trying to protect Julie and me. He said you would have been racing after us."

"Yes, I would, and why not?"

They walked to the end of the crescent and then turned. As they turned Victor dropped Nicky's hand, and, although he had not meant to do so, he did not take it again. They retraced their steps, side by side.

"Do you know what I'm thinking?" Victor asked.

"No, what?"

"I'm wondering what I should do if he was here now, the German boy, and if it was between us as to who should get you."

"Don't be silly, Vic."

"It's far from silly, Nicky. I shouldn't want him to get you."

"But what would you do?"

"I don't know. It would be no good to fight him, but a man ought to think of something."

"You think about business for a change, Vic. We must get back to the poor old Beach Court. She looks so forlorn she makes me feel badly."

"We'll go back and have a sundowner. What do you say, Nicky?"

"All right," she said.

The next morning Julie was down early, and she saw Victor in front of the hotel supervising the filling of the petrol tank. When that operation was finished he spoke to her, and they stood together surveying the square.

"Nicky's been through quite an experience," Julie said after a minute or two.

"I suppose she has."

"Don't let her go off again like that, will you?"

Victor looked at her, wondering what she meant, and finally asked, "Is she really gone on the young German?"

"No, of course not," said Julie.

"Then why should she be tracking off again?"

"Oh, girls are likely to have ideas, you know. Nicky needs to be wanted. She needs to be loved. I wouldn't have said anything, but I'm fond of her."

"I see," said Victor. "But the German is out of it?"

"He's not the sort for her, and she knows that very well

now. Anyway, he's gone for good, and nobody can say where he is."

"I see," Victor said again.

But he puzzled a great deal over these things which Julie had gone out of her way to say to him, and, alone in the private bar that afternoon, he reflected further.

"As near as I can make out," he said to himself, "what she was really communicating was that Nicky is head over heels about young Hitler. Of course she wouldn't admit it, but that's most certainly the only sense you could put into her remarks. Well, I rather suppose I knew it already. What a rum way to have things go!"

19

Hugo and jacob traveled only at night for a while and in one way or another managed to get through the mountains. The place where they walked now was flat and, so far as the eye could see, endless. The drought was on the veld, and the heat eddied from the red-and-ochre earth. The monotony of the landscape was broken only by the isolated hills with flat tops which were set about like some kind of massive and unfinished rustic furniture and, much less frequently, by an occasional village surrounded by windmills and sustaining out of some secret store of moisture a few clusters of trees. As often as not there was no real village at all but only the platform of a railroad station, a signboard with a name, and roads leading off to sheep farms out of sight across the plain. In spite of the drought there was some parched grass, not enough to change the color of the earth, except sometimes far off, or there was at least a sprinkling of gray tussocks which provided forage of a sort for the hungry sheep.

They hid themselves as best they could when the sun was high, usually near some *kopje* not too far removed from the road, for roads were their only guide. When they were hidden in this way, waiting for the dusk to come, Hugo sometimes talked with Jacob.

"What do you think of freedom?" he asked. "Do you think it is pleasant to be free?"

"Yes, baas," said Jacob, smiling. "It is very nice."

But Hugo said to himself bitterly, "How ignorant he is! He is not free and never will be. Whatever freedom may be, and I am not sure that I shall ever understand, he knows nothing at all about it." Then in a little while he reflected further, "But he is happy. I look at him, and he is smiling. Is it because he is so ignorant? That must be the reason. It is because he is of a low order and has a limited intelligence."

So, he said to himself, Nicky was wrong in what she had tried to say, and this was not strange, since she was only a young girl and should not have attempted any flight into such things as philosophy. She was wrong, and there was really no distinction between freedom and the lack of freedom but only between wisdom and ignorance. Hugo felt that he was wise, just as Jacob was ignorant, and here was the important cosmic thing. He had thus, in his own way and with reference to certain arbitrary standards which remained in his mind, refuted Nicky completely. Yet she continued to smile at him. He could see her smiling now, although when last they had parted she had looked at him only in anger. He remembered her rage well enough, with a heavy heart, sometimes with apprehension as of something still unfinished and impending, but it was always Nicky's smile, the tenderness of that smile and sometimes of her voice, which followed Hugo night after night over the veld.

Nicky was with him in the hot sun as he lay on the parched earth; she was with him under the moon and stars; she was with him waking and sleeping. He argued with her, and again and again he refuted her as he had done this first time, but she was always smiling and paying no attention to his logic. Then one day Hugo realized that he did not want Nicky to be wrong; he wanted her to be right, no matter what the cost to himself. His thoughts and his longing were drawing together and working as one.

So far as the flight was concerned, Hugo had no more sense of guilt and especially no more feeling of alarm and pursuit. A kind of stubborn fatalism had taken the place of his former reproaches and fears—this and a tendency to look ahead instead of back. Yet he did not like to face the question of where he was going and of how long he would stay, because as yet he was going nowhere. He postponed the formation of any plan. He cherished an anticipation of some improvement in his fortunes, but instinct told him this anticipation must be vague and general or that it would perish in the drought of reality.

Jacob foraged, but it was hard for him to find enough

for the two of them to eat. Sometimes they had nothing for a day at a time except mealie meal and a little grease. Where it came from Hugo never asked, and he choked it down against his still strong distaste. Often they were thirsty. But in spite of the deprivation and hardship there were times, oftener than before, when the mere fact of being alive and out of doors seemed inexplicably rewarding to Hugo. He did not know what to make of this feeling and feared that he might be going native; therefore he struggled against it and made himself uncomfortable and irritable.

Finally there was a time when it rained. They saw the cloud in the sky when it was far off, shimmering in the heat mist which was in front of their eyes. This cloud seemed to remain just as it was for a long time, but at last they knew it was coming closer. The sky darkened, and they saw lightning and began to hear thunder. They were glad when the rain came, but it was cooler than Hugo had thought it would be and furiously soaking. He had never known so great a flood to fall from the sky. Their resting place near a *kopje* had seemed sheltered, but it did not protect them from the rain, and soon there was water all around. Before the storm stopped evening had almost come, and they could see only a little distance in the wet darkness.

"I think we must walk to someplace where we can build a fire," Hugo said. "I am wet and hungry. I do not like it here."

Jacob went off a little way to look about and then came back.

"There is no way through the river, baas," he said.

Hugo did not believe there was any river at this place which he had observed to be dry and barren.

"Why are you lying to me?" he demanded.

"I am not lying, baas," said Jacob. "There is a river. I will show you the river, baas."

"I know you lie. I will not look," said Hugo.

He shivered all night, and he was angry with Jacob. But this anger itself was guilty and ashamed, for Hugo remembered that he might easily have killed Jacob by this time, had things gone a little differently. Had Dr. Weiss issued orders for Hugo to shoot Jacob at once, instead of bidding him see Nicky, Jacob would without a doubt be dead.

In the morning they walked on. The landscape had changed; it was refreshed and had turned to green, and the air was sweet to breathe.

"There, baas," said Jacob. "The river was there."

He pointed, but Hugo saw nothing. "This time," Hugo said, "I was certainly right. He did lie, and he is lying now." But there was a donga, made in the beginning perhaps by the feet of cattle and long deepened by erosion; looking more closely, Hugo saw in this depression the marks of water and in the bottom little circles of moisture which had not yet disappeared. This was where the great flood of the rain, draining from the area all around, had run off, and indeed there must have been, for the duration of a few hours, a rushing river.

Hugo glanced away from the donga, and they walked on. He was still furious with Jacob, furious with himself.

Finally he said, "There was a river."

The countryside was no longer grotesque and mocking, but there were barriers between him and the satisfaction of the land, just as there were barriers between him and Jacob. He felt himself inadequate, conspired against, and he settled into a morose silence. Soon he found himself thinking of Nicky and trying to remember the sound of her voice.

Jacob kept the patch of cloth he had torn from the sleeve of Hugo's uniform, the patch with the gold-threaded swastika. He did this partly because of his passion for bright things and an instinct for ornamentation and partly because he knew there was plenty of prestige to be acquired from imitation of the customs of the white baas. He was careful not to let Hugo see the swastika, for, although it had been thrown away and had thus come properly into his hands, the white baas was peculiar in many matters and might take offense. But when Jacob went off on foraging or exploring trips he took the emblem from his pocket and pinned it on his tunic—not on the sleeve, for his sleeves were too short, but on his breast or on his back. Once or twice he pinned it on his fez and walked jauntily.

Usually he was seen only by other natives, and he acquired prestige and was envied and admired, which was pleasant beyond most other things. But nevertheless rumors began to fly from farm to farm and from dorp to dorp concerning the strange black Nazi and the spread of the non-European front from Natal. Even those who would have welcomed a movement directed against the English were disquieted by these rumors. One did not necessarily believe what one was told, especially when no one seemed to have seen the black Nazi with his own eyes, but the story was not of a kind to be forgotten. It was of a kind which would grow and spread.

After the rain Hugo and Jacob went into a region where the veld was greener and better, and while Hugo remained in hiding Jacob went to seek what the countryside might offer. As usual, he pinned the swastika conspicuously upon himself, and this time he encountered two Japanese bicycle salesmen who had dismounted from a train and were waiting on a cinder platform beside the tracks. Here there was no town but only a group of station buildings and the signboard bearing the name Westover Road. The road went straight away and vanished in dust. Jacob saw that the Japanese salesmen had taken two or three bicycles out of their crates, and these bicycles were bright and gleaming. He was drawn toward them, and when he stood near the bicycles he lingered.

The two Japanese, both small, smiling men with regular white teeth, were exceedingly dapper. Their clothes were freshly pressed, their shoes shined and, even here, virtually without dust; their collars were white, their ties neatly knotted and matching the handkerchiefs in their breast pockets. When Jacob reached out to touch with his finger the gleaming nickel of the handle bars which had fascinated him, one of the two spoke sharply, and both smiles turned to frowns. But if it had not been for this they might not have noticed what Jacob was wearing on his chest.

The Japanese spoke to one another excitedly in their own language. There was no one who might have met Jacob in this remote spot who had half so keen a sense of world affairs as these two traveled men from the islands of the East. They realized at once that they had come upon something of surpassing importance, something which might be of the liveliest interest at home. Their eyes glittered, and they began smiling again. They agreed instantly on discreet questioning.

"*Wie geht's?*" inquired the one nearest to Jacob in a purring voice.

Jacob did not understand but was pleased with the attention and with the friendly attitude, because the qualities of the bicycles were to some extent attached to the owners of the bicycles, and he seemed to recognize a kinship between this strange greeting and the words Hugo had taught him. He came to a position of attention briskly, and the Japanese exchanged low but excited comments in their own tongue.

"*Sprechen sie Deutsch?*" inquired the same member of the pair. This was formal discourse, but he did not know the German idiom well.

Jacob was still at a loss, but he admired the bicycles and desired to be looked upon with favor. In the absence of any other notion of how to respond, he raised his arm and said, "Heil Hitler!"

The effect was electric. Both Japanese were dispatched

into ecstasies of satisfaction, for their eyes and ears had confirmed what the sight of the swastika upon Jacob's bosom had first indicated.

"Where is your baas?" asked the Japanese who had not yet spoken to Jacob, and the black boy pointed in the general direction in which Hugo lay concealed.

This place of concealment was under a sprawling thorn tree at no great distance from the station platform, the fence which divided the tracks, and the small station buildings. The thorn tree was the largest of several which grew near the foot of a long, low hill, a sort of mound covered with grass and coarser vegetation, which stretched perhaps a quarter of a mile over the veld. At this spot, too, was a deserted building of baked mud, the door and windows open and blank, and two or three wagon wheels and some parts of a windmill lying on the ground.

Having an appreciation of international politics, the two bicycle salesmen knew that it was not for them to interfere in matters of this kind but only to inform themselves and to observe. Having reached this point, therefore, they politely dissociated themselves from Jacob, and he wandered off, more or less recollecting the errands upon which he was supposed to be engaged. The alert Japanese eyes followed him.

"We must see more of this," one of the salesmen said to the other.

Jacob did not proceed far at the time, for beyond the end of the station platform he found two black girls sitting upon some bundles, waiting. The name of one of these girls was Emmy, and he found it possible to make conversation with her. It was true that he hoped to obtain provender from her or through her aid, but it was also true that mutual admiration was quick to develop. Jacob's own status in this land which the black race had lost but the white race had not yet fully won was so unusual that he had found little opportunity for requited love. His was a half-world, neither one thing nor another, and in Emmy he found a kindred spirit. He lingered in her company for a long time.

Atlee Hinton's farm was on this part of the veld, the first farm along the straight reach of Westover Road. When he returned from Lady Elsie, having completed his arrangements about cattle, he made it a point to talk with all the boys on his place on the subject of Nazi propaganda. When he had said to Julie that he intended to take this menace seriously he had ventured no exaggeration. He was a man of conviction and of loyalties easily aroused. He lost no time in explaining to his own farm people how they might be imposed upon by evil men who would make all kinds of false statements and false promises. He considered this no more than putting them on their guard. It also enabled him to make sure he would be informed if the Nazi serpent should creep near.

Now his zeal was rewarded, for he had identified the crooked cross as the emblem of the secret enemy, and the crooked cross had made its appearance at Westover Road. There was more coming and going than usual that day, because there were two trains, and the Japanese salesmen were transacting business. The report of the black Nazi spread from tongue to tongue, and in a surprisingly short time it had reached the brusque and shaggy man in tweed. Atlee Hinton took down his rifle which in past years had killed big game. He rode for his nearest neighbor, a man named Cradock, who also owned a rifle. The two men, armed and ready, turned toward the railroad with grim faces.

Long before evening they found Jacob, for he was walking along the road with Emmy and the other girl, and he made no effort to conceal himself or to evade them.

They said to him, "Who sent you here?"

"The white baas," said Jacob.

"Where is your white baas?"

Jacob pointed.

"Lead on, boy," said Atlee Hinton. "We have business with your baas."

Jacob led on. He was afoot, and the two men were mounted on horses. He walked ahead, and they came immediately in the rear. This procedure was inconvenient but not upsetting to Jacob, for his conscience was untroubled, and he knew of no precedent for any ill eventuality. If there was something he himself had done the white baas Hugo would explain and make things right. But the chances were that the men were friends of the baas Hugo, and that was good, because the neighborhood was a pleasant one in which to stay. It was Emmy's neighborhood.

They crossed the railroad above the station and followed the tracks on the other side, and presently they came near the thorn trees and the deserted building. Still they did not see Hugo.

Jacob peered ahead anxiously. There seemed to be no one. But then a moment later he understood why. Hugo was lying on the ground under the tree, sound asleep, and did not hear them approaching. The men on the horses halted and looked down.

"He's our man," Cradock said. "There's no mistaking his nationality."

"It's not the one I expected," said Hinton, whose mind had been set on Dr. Weiss. "However, he may lead us to someone else."

The two spoke in low tones and dismounted silently. They walked toward Hugo, leaning down to reach under the tree, and Hinton held his rifle ready. Jacob mistook this gesture, for, although the rifle was held in readiness, Hinton was not intending to shoot Hugo in his sleep. He might have prodded the boy with the barrel in order to wake him, but what he wanted most was to ask some highly important questions.

Mistaking the indication of the rifle, Jacob for the first time became aware of danger. He understood the situation and then a little more than understood. His mind flashed back to an occasion which had been almost exactly like this. It was a scene he had witnessed—nay, in which he himself had participated, as he now thought—in the motion picture of Tarzan. His vision leaped ahead of the present facts into the realm of adventure. He threw back his head and opened his lips to send forth a frightful howl, half animal and half human, which was his version of the memorable call of the moving picture.

Hugo woke and saw the two men. Their horses reared, frightened by Jacob's long howl which was now repeated. Hugo sprang up while Hinton and Cradock tried to control their horses and at the same time reach into the thorns. They were fairly caught for a minute or two, being somewhat entangled and at the same time occupied with the frightened horses. Hugo ran around the deserted building and after a moment's hesitation climbed through the window at the rear, waiting until he heard the two men moving about on foot, leading their horses.

"Which way did he go?" Cradock asked.

"He'll head for the hill," said Hinton, "but he hasn't got far yet. He's hiding, and if we beat about here we'll flush him out directly."

Hugo left the building through the door and flattened himself against the outside wall. The two men walked together from the rear to the front and looked in at the door, finding the place empty. He heard one of them poke about in the dark corners while the other held the horses outside.

"Not here," a voice said.

"You go right, and I'll go left," said Hinton, and this suggestion was followed.

They walked separately around the building and met at the rear. By that time Hugo had climbed in through the back window again and was squatting inside.

"He's going to dodge from one bit of cover to another— that's what he's up to," said Hinton.

"Smooth article," said Cradock shortly. "We must flush him in a hurry, or he'll get away."

They beat about behind the wagon wheels and the windmill parts and then around and under the thorn trees and through the tussocks of bush and grass behind which a man might have found some concealment. They visualized Hugo crawling on his belly like a snake, working away from them toward the hill, and they fanned out and made an orderly search, leading their horses so that they could mount instantly if need be.

Hugo waited as long as he dared, for he was sure they would return soon rather than go on blindly without a clue, farther and farther. He looked from the window and saw that they were facing away from him. He took this chance and raced as fast as he could for the railroad station. He reached the platform which was nearest and rounded the corner of the main station building. Several figures were standing at the far end of the opposite platform, but there was no one who seemed to have been attracted by his rapid dash. He listened and heard no sound of pursuit. If he managed reasonably well he was safe. He could escape.

Then he knew, without any doubt, that there was a reason why he might not be able to escape. Jacob was unaccounted for, and he could not leave Jacob. There had been that time when he had readily agreed in sentencing Jacob to death. Sometimes since, walking beside the black boy in the cool nights, he had felt the guilt of blood. He seemed to be walking with a ghost of a human being but, for the grace of God, murdered by his own hand. And then as he recovered from this feeling he had come to look upon Jacob as a sign to Nicky, a hostage of some other life and liberty placed in his keeping. He and Jacob were both of the hunted, and never again could he consider Jacob's life unimportant.

Jacob would have come to no harm now if Hugo had deserted him, but Hugo did not know that. He stood there, his safety ebbing away with the seconds, and still did not consider abandoning the black boy.

He called out, not too loudly, "Jacob!"

Inwardly he cursed Jacob's stupidity and felt that he could beat him for having disappeared. In five minutes perhaps the horsemen with the rifles would be coming back. In three. In two. They would shoot rather than let him get away.

"Jacob!"

The figures at the far end of the platform seemed to turn and stare. That made the danger greater, but Hugo waited. He conceived that the black boy would be helpless in the toils, accused of the sins of the white baas, and in such straits he would not leave him.

Then suddenly Jacob came, in a flash, as if he were riding the wind. He was mounted on one of the Japanese bicycles, and he was pedaling for dear life. He called out as he passed, and although Hugo could not understand the words this made no material difference. Hugo broke cover and ran the length of the platform toward the gleam of nickel plate. In hardly more than another minute he had taken a bicycle also and was riding fast after Jacob, and the two of them receded from the station of Westover Road, clouded in the dust of the veld.

A little later than this Hinton and Cradock paused for a few words with the bicycle salesmen.

"Did somebody steal your bicycles?" they inquired.

"No, thank you, I don't think so," said one of the Japanese politely, and the other said, "Or if they did, I am sure that we will be paid for them."

He smiled so brightly that Hinton and Cradock thought he was being obtuse, but he felt himself clever, for in his pocket he had the gold-threaded swastika which he had received from Jacob's hand. It seemed to him and his colleague that this emblem, in proof of the information they had acquired so unexpectedly, was likely to mean a great deal to them when their accounts were handed in. The possibilities were most interesting.

"Damn it," said Hinton as he and Cradock walked away. "We may search the hill, but we'll not find him. I should have taken a shot at him without waiting."

"Right," said Cradock, "and so should I."

"Sorry we lost the native boy too," said Hinton. "With decent treatment I could have made something of him, I don't doubt. We don't need to let the Nazis win these people. Decent treatment, that's our weapon."

"Yes, and shooting on sight for any Nazi agents who are stirring them up."

There was that kind of intensity about both men which admitted of no doubt as to the earnestness of their resolve and the determination with which it would be carried out.

20

THE ROADS ACROSS THE VELD were dusty and corrugated, so that they made one's teeth chatter, but Hugo and Jacob did not mind this or the fact that their clothes were filled with the fine red earth. The dust reduced them to a single color, and their spirits joined in the pleasure of the level track and the speed of the wheels which emancipated them from former burdens which had tied them to place and time. The warm air becoming cool with motion, the countryside streaming past, the horizon always coming up ahead and going down behind—all these renewed them and turned them into carefree adventurers.

But Hugo asked himself, "Where am I going now? And why?"

When they rested beside the road his eyes followed the surface of the ground where the level veld rose into a bare slope which was not red nor orange, but tawny, a curious streak of color in the sunlight.

"It is like Nicky's hair," he said to himself. "It is like her hair when she is out of doors. . . . It even glistens like her hair. I know what I want. All I want is Nicky. I do not care about anything else."

But he felt sad, because he still suspected that this was a very great weakness on his part and that it was unbecoming in a young man of his principles, assuming he could ever decide what his principles now were. Deliberately he closed this line of thought, because he was not ready to face any sober implications and he had no desire to begin inventorying his conscience and his duties. All that sort of thing was lofty but boring.

He felt sad, too, because Nicky hated him and because he had shut himself off from her. It did not seem that he could have done the things he knew he had done; it seemed that someone else must have been that person.

When it was cooler he and Jacob got on their wheels and were off again, and the ridges in the drought-stricken road made their bones jounce and quiver, but they did not mind.

One morning they came to a town with trees and pleasant streets, but the streets were utterly deserted, and the place was as quiet as if it had been imperiously and supernaturally hushed. There was nothing in nature so mute and motionless, Hugo thought, and he was uneasy for fear that some tragedy, some collective trance might lie here around him. Wonderingly, with awe, he looked this way and that as he led Jacob into the town, and not a living person did he see. The neat houses stood as if their occupants had ceased to exist, or at least to breathe, and the empty streets and sidewalks appeared as if they might never resound to foot-beat or motor horn again. Since there was no breeze, the leaves of the trees were suspended and at rest.

Could there have been a sudden plague, Hugo wondered? What sudden rushing forth or paralyzing spell could have left this eloquent emptiness and silence? He turned to Jacob, who was following him at a few paces.

"What is the reason for this?" he asked. "There is not a soul to be seen or heard. . . . But I warn you, I will not listen to any nonsense about a white princess or a mighty hunter! I want only truth."

"Baas, I can tell you."

"Tell me then."

"It is Sunday, baas."

There was no church bell ringing, but Hugo knew how the bells would sound in this waiting air, through these hushed streets and squares; he knew now that the town was not sleeping or dead but only ready in the holiness of the day for the call to church and chapel. Behind the closed doors and shining windows were men, women, and children donning their Sunday clothes, and all life was decent and quiet against the call of the bells.

He could not help laughing aloud at the absurdity of his own qualms, and this laughter was pleasant and happy. It seemed to him that he had not laughed so gently, yet so freely, in many years. Jacob laughed, too, and that helped, since there is so often a need for laughter to be shared. Then they leaned their bicycles against a wall and waited until the church bells rang and the worshipers walked through the town.

Near the end of the town was a large park, and they went there and saw a girl in a pretty Sunday frock lying on the grass while she played records on a portable phonograph. Hugo sat on a bench at a little distance and listened for a long time, as if he had been a member of an audience at some fine concert. He pretended that the girl was Nicky and that he and she were listening together. He had forgotten how strange he must look in his shrunken checked suit discolored by dust, and he thought only of the music for which he was thirsty as one may be when a long time deprived. The girl played part of Schubert's "Unfinished Symphony," Von Weber's "Invitation to the Waltz," and Debussy's "Clair de Lune." Hugo was quite lost, and he did not wish the music to end, but after a while the girl gathered up her things, closed the phonograph into a satchel, and went away through the trees.

"I have thought of this as a wild country," Hugo said to himself, "but now I know that it is full of towns like this, with church bells and green parks, music to hear and books to read, traffic signals, and health regulations duly posted. How different from what I thought!"

He looked for Jacob and had some trouble in finding him, for the black boy had fallen asleep under the shrubbery. Again they walked through the town, neglecting any caution as to who might see them, and presently passed a build-

ing which was designated as the public library. It stood near
the park, and Hugo looked hard, because he had not read
a book in a long time. But the library was closed on Sunday, and, even if it had been open, he possessed no money
with which to become a subscriber.

"This might become my salvation," he thought. "Books
are for the purpose of instructing and improving, and no
one needs instruction or improvement more than I at this
moment. What is more, I must face the problem of the
future. I must be willing to confront the questions which
I have been avoiding and to supply answers. But I cannot
go into the library, and therefore I cannot make use even
of these printed counselors. . . ."

Just the same, he kept on reflecting and thinking how
much he might profit by the writings of great men who
in their time had solved problems as serious as his. Long
after dark he left Jacob asleep and went back to the library
alone. He found a window unlocked and forced an entrance. Soon he was standing in front of the bookshelves,
trying to read the titles in the shaft of moonlight from over
his shoulder. Most of these titles were strange to him and
seemed to suggest no useful application to his own need.
Whatever he was looking for he was not finding. He felt
let down and disappointed and decided to leave the way he
had come, but then his eye fell on the back of a thick
book and its title, *War and Peace*.

He had never heard of this book, but he took it from the
shelf at once, thinking that it must contain the strength and

wisdom of which he was in need. He was resolved to carry
the volume with him and to return it when he had finished.
This decision was not difficult to put into effect, and when
he slept that night the book was beside him.

The next day he read, and felt the shadow of Napoleon
across the years. When he came to the scenes of campaign-
ing and of battle he was fascinated and turned page after
page with breathless attention. Then, fully absorbed, he
reached the scene where Prince Andrey lay wounded on
the field of Austerlitz, and through the eyes of the prince
he seemed to look up at the heavens.

Above him there was nothing but the sky—the lofty sky, not
clear, but still immeasurably lofty, with great clouds creeping
quietly over it. "How quietly, peacefully and triumphantly,
and not like us running, shouting and fighting . . . how differently are those clouds creeping over that lofty, limitless sky.
How was it I did not see that lofty sky before? And how happy
I am to have found it at last. Yes! All is vanity, all is a cheat,
except that infinite sky. There is nothing, nothing but
that . . ."

Hugo read the words again and again and then closed
the book and lay upon the ground. It seemed to him that
he was no longer what he had been. He was free. He had
escaped. He looked at Jacob and remembered how often
he had seen the black boy peering into the sky overhead,
how on that first morning on the height above Port Quentin
Jacob had gazed at the clouds, and Hugo himself had been
able to see nothing. . . .

"All this time he has known something that I have not,"

Hugo said to himself. "I said he was not free, but he was free, and I did not have the wit to know it."

Yet what had happened in his own mind Hugo could not have told, except that Nicky had been right, and freedom had needed to be won there. Ripened and prepared by so much which had gone before, Hugo had emerged through vexations and doubts into the open, into the clear.

"Come," Hugo said to Jacob, "we are going back to the place we left behind so long ago. There is no time to lose."

He had left the book on the library steps after dark, and now it was the early morning of another day.

"Yes, baas," said Jacob, and then as they were getting their bicycles ready he went on, "Baas, what was that place where the men came with guns?"

"Westover Road."

"I think it would be very good to go there," Jacob said, for he was thinking of Emmy, the black girl.

"No," said Hugo, "it would be very foolish. We are going to Port Quentin."

"Not to Westover Road, baas?"

"No."

Now they were on their wheels again, off over the veld in the early morning, and, although they were only returning whence they had come, the spirit of adventure was stronger than it had been before.

21

Victor tolley heard someone enter the hotel at the front door, and he went downstairs hopefully, because if there was a new arrival he would not be obliged to spend the rest of the morning over his books as he had, with much distaste, resolved to do. The man he saw waiting at the desk in the office was a strange-looking customer and entirely unfamiliar. Victor was disappointed, because this was certainly no prospective guest. More likely a stray cat about to ask for a bit of assistance of some material kind.

"What can I do for you?" Victor inquired, with the distinct intimation that he hoped nothing much would be required. Then he saw the newcomer's face clearly and exclaimed, "Oh lord!"

"Good morning," said Hugo, smiling.

"Come, this won't do! You must keep out of sight, you know. Come inside here with me before anyone catches on."

"No," said Hugo, "please do not trouble yourself about me."

"Oh! Aren't you afraid?"

"No."

"Haven't been pardoned or something, have you?"

"No."

"I see. Well! You do look thin, and you could do with a haircut. It gives me a queer feeling to be seeing you again like this, and it will take a minute or so to get over it. I was thinking not long ago what I should do if you turned up again."

Hugo laughed and asked what Victor had thought of doing and whether he had made up his mind.

"Not altogether," said Victor slowly, "but I was getting on to an idea. I suppose what you're really after is to see Nicky, isn't it?"

"Why you should think that I don't know," said Hugo, "but it is true. However, I am glad to see you, because you did your best to help me, and now I can thank you."

"Don't mention it," said Victor. "It's what a man can do in emergencies that counts, you see." Inwardly he added, "And this is an emergency right now, if I ever saw one. I must keep my wits about me, that's certain." Aloud he went on, "Nicky's off with the Williamses just at present —gone fishing since right after breakfast."

"They are still here, then—the Williamses?"

"Yes. You're not glad of that?"

"I did not mean to give that impression. I should like to wait for Nicky. Except for that I will not trouble you."

"How stiff he talks for a young one!" thought Victor. "But there's something about him—you can see it in his eye." He said to Hugo, "Yes, of course you're to wait, but don't talk of troubling me. Will you sign the register, or had you better not? I mean, in case of someone looking for you?"

"I would not care, except that I have no money. I am sorry. I will sit down and wait here."

"You're quite sure it's safe for you to be about? You don't think you'd better be moving along, in case there's a pursuit out after you? You may have been seen, you know. I can give a message to Nicky for you."

"I am not afraid of any pursuit. I will wait."

"I hope you're doing the wise thing," said Victor with a dubious tone. "There've been some strangers lurking about the place of late, just the type for undercover men. Very well, if you're determined to risk it, which I'm sure I shouldn't do in your position, you'd best have a room. No, no! I insist. Nicky wouldn't like it if I didn't look after you properly after all you must have been through."

"I do not think she would care," said Hugo. "Perhaps she will not like it if you take me in. I am not sure that she will let me speak to her."

"You think she has it in for you?"

"I am not sure what you mean. I gave her reason to think badly of me."

"In that case hadn't you better be off now, before she comes?"

"No. The reason I have come here is to see Nicky."

"I see. Well, it's what I thought. Come along upstairs, and after you've had a tub and got into some presentable clothes you can tell me what's been happening to you and where you've been. I'm sorry to say the German navy came and lifted everything you'd left behind, but I have some things you can have, and welcome."

As he said this Victor was thinking that he would not care to face Nicky if he had done anything less for young Becker.

"I do not know how to thank you enough. I have no right to expect such kindness."

"Not a word!" said Victor. "You see, I've a curiosity to find out all about you. We'll have time while we're waiting for the others to come back." He was thinking to himself, "I've got to have something to go on. Otherwise there's no telling what to do. It's ridiculous to think of fighting a chap like him, but there must be something left to a man in my position."

While Hugo was bathing Victor took the suit which had once belonged to Thomas Hickey and prepared to dispose of it, but at the back door of the Beach Court he saw Jacob, returned after many days. For the moment he had forgotten about Jacob, and he beheld him with much gratification.

"So it's you! Well, you've had a bit of wandering about and, I daresay, plenty of hunting and all that. Now what you must do is settle down. I hope you understand what I mean."

"Yes, baas," said Jacob.

"You're to start in directly with your old work. You see, I've been expecting to see you back one of these days. A boy like you has a future if he's willing to settle down and stay in one place as he should. No more trekking!"

"No, baas," said Jacob, grinning pleasantly.

"No. That's very good. I believe you do understand. Stay in one place, work hard, and you'll get along. That's the ticket, you see. Someday you can be a waiter. I know very well you'd like to be a proper waiter—any boy would. Now, mind you, do what I say."

"Yes, baas," said Jacob. "It is very good to stay in one place and work hard."

As Victor made his way back through the hotel, his major problem still weighing upon his mind, he reflected idly that the native problem was not so difficult, really, if one applied good common sense. Consider Jacob, now, a primitive native if there ever was one, yet turning into a useful boy with something ahead of him besides sleeping in the sun. Victor also reflected that he would like to have Jacob's version of the expedition with Hugo Becker and that it was too bad this was out of the question.

If Victor had glanced through the window then he would have seen Jacob putting on Mr. Hickey's old trousers and coat over his own khaki tunic and shorts. Jacob seemed pleased to be clad in this manner, and the truth was that the suit fitted him better than it had fitted Hugo.

On his way upstairs Victor picked up a copy of the Natal *Advertiser* and considered carefully. His eyes narrowed, and he began to smile. He went to the room where Hugo was dressing and sat on the bed.

"I daresay you haven't seen the papers much," he said.

"No."

"Did you know," Victor asked, "that the Germans have gone into Austria?"

Hugo turned in surprise and stared at the headlines in the newspaper Victor was holding.

"You see, Hitler's in Vienna," Victor went on. "He's made a roaring great speech, and this is what he says: 'Whatever happens, the German Reich as it stands today shall never be broken by anyone again and shall never be torn apart. No suffering, no force can violate this oath sworn today by German men from Königsberg to Cologne, from Hamburg to Vienna.' What do you think of that?"

"I don't know," said Hugo. "I am surprised. I wonder if the Austrians wanted the *Anschluss*."

"Not much, by the look of the thing. You should see your face. Took you a bit sudden, didn't it? Makes you want to be back home, I expect."

"Perhaps. I don't really know, you see. I was thinking about the Austrians, wondering how they feel. I have been in Vienna. Yes, I have had good times in Vienna."

"But you are German."

"Yes, but to be a German one does not have to stop being first of all a man." Hugo leaned upon the window sill and looked out, and, as he had hoped, he could see the sky above the mountain in back of the town. He looked earnestly into that distant and brilliant sky, until tears came into his eyes. After a while he turned again and said, "Do not think I am not a patriot. I hope I shall always be a patriot. If I were in Germany, where, no doubt, there is great cheering on every side, who knows what I should feel? But I am not there, and it is doubtful if I shall ever be there again. I am here, and because of what I have felt and suffered and what I have learned I think of the Austrians and all that this news may mean to them. A man is different after he has had to run with the hares, not only out of doors but in his own mind."

Victor found nothing to say at the moment, but he was thinking, "Well, I didn't make so much out of that, now, did I?"

When Hugo had finished dressing himself in some of Victor's clothes, which fitted him loosely, he allowed himself to be taken to the dining room, which was otherwise deserted, and there he waited while Victor arranged for him to be served. The two sat at a table together, and Hugo told Victor a great deal, but by no means all, about the events which had occurred since the beginning of the first flight from Port Quentin. Victor was particularly interested in Dr. Weiss and in the story that Julie Williams was a British agent.

"You don't like Mrs. Williams much, do you?" he asked Hugo.

The German boy shrugged.

"Is it a fact that she's a confidential agent, do you think?"

"I do not care. It makes no difference. I do not think about it any more."

"Still, if she happened to be one—and of course I'm not saying she is—if she happened to be one, and you were to give information about her in the proper quarter, well, it might put you in right again?"

Hugo shrugged as he had done before.

"I only mention the chance," said Victor. "A man in your situation has to take matters between his fingers. He can't be squeamish, I shouldn't think. After all, if she got you into the mess, it would be a way of her getting you out of it."

Hugo said something, but his mouth was full of bread, and Victor did not understand. They sat on in silence, and Victor thought there might be something here to serve the purpose he had formed in his active mind. There must be, he believed, a plan for everything, and a man must be able to do something for himself, whether the man happened to be Hugo Becker or Victor Tolley, and no matter what the occasion, merely one of life and death or one concerning the stakes of love.

Victor was in the bar when Eric, Julie, and Nicky drove up in front of the Beach Court. He ambled out to meet them and watched as they took their things out of the automobile.

"What's got into you, Vic?" Nicky asked. "You look as if you knew something."

"Heigh ho, Tolley!" said Eric good-naturedly. "There's

nothing like having an open face that a young girl can read like a book."

Victor smiled, looking very wide awake, his hair stringing down over his forehead, and a boyish twisting of his lips, but he would not disclose anything until he was able to take Nicky aside, alone.

"He's upstairs, on the balcony. He's keeping out of sight, waiting for you."

"Who?"

"Hugo Becker, the German chap."

Nicky stood looking blankly into Victor's face.

"I don't think I can see him, Vic. No, I can't. You must tell him."

"But will he mind what I say? He won't be inclined to take a no for an answer," Victor said. "You could see him and send him off, couldn't you?"

"When did he come? What does he want?"

Victor told her briefly all that had happened during her absence. She listened and even made some comments, and then she found herself going up the stairs, thinking over and over that she ought not to see him, that nothing could come of her ever seeing him again. As she reached the top of the stairs she could look through the passage to the balcony, and Hugo was standing there, looking neat and clean and somewhat lost in Victor's clothes.

"Nicky!" he said. "Nicky, I had to see you."

He did not attempt to come close to her, and she said, "Why, Hugo? Don't you understand it's no good?"

"I have so much to tell you, things I want you to know. You were right in what you said to me. I know now how right you were. I do not want to die for anything, Nicky. I want to live."

She kept looking at him, but she did not speak.

"I used to think life was meant only to be sacrificed, but that is not so. Death may happen, but it is not the purpose. Life itself is the purpose, and except for you I should never have found out this important truth. You see, Nicky, I have fought for freedom in my own head, and I have had such fine help—you have helped me, and that native boy, Jacob, has helped me. . . ."

"I am glad of what you say," Nicky found herself saying at last, "but what is to come of all this?"

"You do not believe in me, Nicky?"

"No, I won't say that, but I'll never be sure whether I believe in you or not, and that's the most dreadful thing of all. I'm glad you're looking so well, Hugo, honestly I am. You are thin, but you seem well, and you haven't that fanatical look. Your face isn't sharp and cruel the way it was. . . ."

She seemed unable to stop looking at him, and her look was an earnest examination, a probing under which he gave ground. Whether he blushed or not was hard to tell, because he was so burned by the sun and wind. She started to ask whether he was not in danger, to have come back to Port Quentin this way, openly, but she checked herself, because she thought of the last time they had met and how he had pretended to be in danger when really he was not. There it was again, the awkwardness, the distrust which stood between them.

"You look lovelier than ever and younger," he said to her.

"I've been fishing, or pretending to. We didn't catch anything, but we had a good time."

"I like to fish too."

They were saying silly, conventional things, and each knew the conversation had become of no importance whatever, that there was no real communication from one to the other. They had gone on in this way for a while when they were interrupted by a native boy from downstairs bringing a folded paper which he handed to Hugo. Hugo read what was written and put the paper into his pocket. Nicky could not tell whether the message had been good or bad news; all she knew was that Hugo had been incited to some action.

"Will you excuse me?" he asked. "There is something of importance. I will come back as soon as I can."

He went through the passage, along the hall, and then she heard him retrace his steps and go down the stairs. She was puzzled to know what he could be doing or where he could be going. She was still on the balcony, wondering, when Victor came.

"Where has Hugo gone?" she asked.

"I'll know in a few minutes," he said, "and then I can tell you."

"Who could have known he was here? Who sent him a message?"

"I sent it to him," said Victor. "Would you like to read it? This is a copy."

He handed her a paper, and in his untidy handwriting she read the words: "Dr. Weiss is at the turn of the river road. He is bound to get you, no matter what. If you put up some information on Julie Williams you can set yourself right for good. There's no other chance, you can be sure."

Nicky did not understand. She looked from the paper to Victor's face.

"It's all fair and square," he said. "Of course there's no Dr. Weiss anywhere about, you see. It's only a test, and the reason it's fair and square is that if he goes looking for Dr. Weiss, in order to save himself that way, he isn't worthy of you, now, is he? I know how you feel about him, Nicky. He's more to you than I am, and this was all I could think of to do. I told you before that it's no good fighting a chap over a girl, because even if you win, where are you? But you can make the other chap show what he's made of. When he read the note he believed it, all right. I know because of the way he rushed about. It's up to him now whether he turns out good or bad, you see."

Nicky leaned against the balcony railing, feeling frail and small.

"He didn't leave by the front door," she said.

"He wouldn't have gone that way," said Victor, "not to make the shortest time to the river road."

"Do you think that's where he's gone?—to the river road?"

"I don't know. Do you?"

"I don't know, either, Vic."

"If he has, have I got a chance, Nicky? It will be his fault, won't it? And you couldn't care for the kind who would be an informer to save his skin, and all the rest?"

"You're all right, Vic," she said firmly but in a voice she thought might choke her. "I'm glad you did what you did. Now I'll know. I won't have to wonder, wonder, wonder. I think it would have driven me mad. This is the same thing that happened before, the same thing all over again. You did well to think of it, Vic, really you did very well."

"How many minutes, I wonder," said Vic, looking at his watch. "Seems to me he must have gone to the river road. He did hate Julie Williams from the start, you know."

"Yes, I know."

"But you don't have to judge him yet, Nicky."

"I can't help thinking what I have to think," she said. "Where else could he be? Where else?"

"I don't know," said Victor, "but there's one other chance. It's not certain yet, though I wish it was. You said yourself you had to be sure."

"I'm afraid I am sure already," said Nicky, "because I have been through this before."

"Perhaps he'll change his mind and turn back," Victor said.

And then there was a commotion downstairs, and in a

great rush Julie and Hugo came piling up and through the passage to the balcony. Eric was following them.

"I don't understand this," Julie said. "Hugo found me on the beach and showed me this note to put me on my guard. Is the Weiss man really here? Is that unpleasant spy story coming up again? If it is, what do you think I should do?"

Eric said, "I don't like this business, Tolley. Why do you have to write notes containing my wife's name?"

Victor began to explain, but they paid scant attention to him, because Nicky was crying so strangely.

"Hugo, Hugo!" she cried out, and he took her in his arms in front of them all and kissed her.

"You see," said Victor slowly and sadly, "that's what it was all about. It was fair and square, and I couldn't think of anything else, though if there'd been more time I might have done much better. I hoped he'd go to the river road—of course I did—but it would have been his doing, not anybody else's. He didn't go. He went to do the right thing instead, and so I'm dished, but I would have been dished in any case, it turns out. Nobody can say I didn't try. I suppose I'm not the romantic sort. I'm the practical kind, good at business and at meeting emergencies of one sort or another. . . ."

Hugo was not yet clear, by any means, and seemed to think that Dr. Weiss was to arrive momentarily. But Nicky led him away, along the balcony.

"I don't understand," he said. "Is it because I am German that I cannot understand all this? But I do not care, for you have forgiven me, Nicky. I came to take you with me if I could. We can make a start together somehow, I know, for I have seen your country, and it is so new and full of room. I will be a farmer—I will tend sheep or cattle—I will be or do anything for you, because I love you, Nicky, my darling. I have nothing to offer you now, but I want you to marry me."

By this time they were alone on the balcony, and the afternoon was far gone. They could hear the sea, and the slanting sunlight crept under the big tree in the square in front of the hotel. Nicky put her hand upon Hugo's hair, and the gesture was a kind of taking of possession.

"I will marry you," she said.

For a long time they were together on the balcony, and although they had so much to tell to one another they could bring themselves to speak few words. In silence they exchanged the only priceless confidences, their arms intertwined, her cheek against his shoulder, her hair touching his lips, and their eyes looking ahead into the long future.

In the end they stood at the doorway of Nicky's room, and Hugo said curiously, "So this is where you live. This is where you have been all the long nights when I have thought of you."

"You have seen this room before, Hugo."

"No, when? When could I have seen it?"

"Don't you remember that first morning? I was doing my exercises. . . ."

"So it was you, Nicky. It was not Mrs. Williams. Then there is no reason at all why I did not like her! I wonder if I will ever come to the last of my mistakes."

"You didn't think it was Julie? You didn't!"

"I am afraid that I did."

Nicky laughed, and all he could do to cover his embarrassment was to kiss her again and again to make her stop
laughing.

That evening Julie remarked to Eric, "Doesn't it surprise you to find that Nicky is so wise a person? I envy her,
you know, because she has the faculty of seeing things
simply, as they really are. That's a rare faculty, and I've
never seen it before, I think. If I had perhaps I should have
recognized it and saved myself some needless worry. But
you and I can get something out of it, at our time of life,
if we admit that the world is often a plain and simple place
and not, as we're so used to thinking it, an unmitigated web
of intrigue."

Eric grunted, and Julie went on talking. So it happened
that Nicky was to Julie at the end almost precisely what
Julie had been to Nicky at the beginning.

Somewhat later Julie asked, "What do you think will
happen to Victor Tolley?"

"I fancy he'll stagger on," said Eric. "You can't down
his kind. Just now he's got some tickets in the Rhodesian
lottery, and as soon as he puts his hands on his winnings
he's going to build an outdoor swimming bath. I may as
well say I like Tolley tremendously. He's the apotheosis
of the unsuccessful business man, that's what he is, and,
like all his type, he has unbounded confidence and, when
you come right down to it, the most amazing interest in
everything except business."

The most extraordinary aspect of Victor Tolley's test was that Dr. Karl Weiss was actually approaching Port Quentin at the very time the test was put into effect. Dr. Weiss was coming down from the hills in order to begin systematically at the beginning, where he should have started in the first instance, to follow through the affair of Hugo Becker. He was driving a small and, in some respects, a ridiculous automobile called a "D.K.W." The letters stood for the words, *Das Kleine Wunder*, which is to say "The Little Wonder," and the car had some characteristics which justified the name, as, for instance, the capacity to make forty-five miles on a gallon of petrol and the fact that in place of the gearshift lever there was a crank coming out of the instrument panel, so that the driver appeared constantly—in the hill country—to be winding the mechanism up as if it had been a gigantic clock on wheels.

Dr. Weiss had planned to register at the Beach Court, and he confidently expected to make everyone there uncomfortable, but before he reached the hotel he saw Jacob in the street carrying a basket of vegetables. He recognized Jacob, whom he had never seen, because there was no doubt whatever concerning the coat and pants of the late Thomas Hickey. Dr. Weiss's eyes expressed joy. He parked the D.K.W. and, being careful to attract as little attention as possible, drew Jacob privately to one side, around a corner and behind a tree.

In order to make certain of his identification he extended his hand and said, "Heil Hitler!" a rite to which Jacob promptly responded in kind.

"I do not ask you to tell me where your baas is," said Dr. Weiss. "I know he is far away from here. But there is no harm if you take me to him, is there?"

"No, baas," said Jacob.

"You know where he is now?"

"Yes, baas."

"You trekked a long way with him?"

"Oh yes, baas, many days."

"But we can go to him very easily, because I have a car. Do you like to ride in a motorcar?"

"Yes, baas," said Jacob, and the prospect caused him to grin broadly.

"Good. You will go with me now. There is no need to delay."

Jacob deserted his basket of vegetables without compunction and climbed into the seat of the D.K.W. beside Dr. Weiss.

"Where must I drive first?" inquired the doctor.

He studied the black boy closely, for this was the all-important question. Jacob was aware of its importance, too, and bethought himself what to say. He yearned toward Emmy, the girl who had shown herself ready to be charmed by him.

"Westover Road, baas," said Jacob.

"Good!" said Dr. Weiss. "We will go quietly, because it is best if no one sees us here."

Jacob had been considerably depressed that day by Victor Tolley's lecture on the advantages of staying in one place and working hard. The prospect of being on the

move again was one to set his spirits aflame. It turned out
that Dr. Weiss had been somewhat oversanguine as to the
possibility of leaving Port Quentin quietly, considering the
nature of the D.K.W., but he coaxed its two cylinders as
expertly as possible. Soon they were driving along the river
road toward the sunset and the cool evening.

Jacob was glad, because he had a tryst to keep at Westover Road. And Dr. Weiss had a tryst to keep also, one
which the fates had made for him, with two grim men
named Hinton and Cradock, one of whom was certain to
recognize, as quickly as the doctor himself, the suit worn
by Mr. Hickey. Although he was not an admirable character, no one could say that Thomas Hickey did not deserve to be avenged. The D.K.W. rattled and shook, and
Dr. Weiss wound it with the crank to change gears, and,
altogether, it was an absurd conveyance in which to drive,
like Jacob, to a lady love, or, like Dr. Weiss, to retribution.

22

❖❖❖❖❖

THE WHOLE AFFAIR of Hugo Becker and his desertion from the *Schleswig-Holstein* was an extremely simple one from the standpoint of those who were able to view everyday events plainly and naturally, but in the official reports dispatched to Germany through one channel and another it became amazingly complicated. There was one set of official documents which insisted that no one had left the German cruiser in South Africa and that her personnel was intact when she sailed homeward. The preliminary reports of Dr. Karl Weiss tended to confirm this view, for it had been the doctor's task to make the facts coincide with the records—often a highly desirable function of government —and he had ventured to put down, as already accomplished, a number of things still remaining to be concluded,

271

although in his mind the conclusion was foregone. Since Dr. Weiss disappeared suddenly and was never heard from again, he could neither retract nor qualify what he had written.

Usually sagacious, the doctor had been strangely impressed by some of the stories told to him by Jacob, the native boy who had been his companion on that last journey, and he transmitted to his superiors from places en route certain information, as he considered it, which led them to spend much time and money on fruitless searches in Tanganyika and other parts of Africa. If they had been more fully advised they could have found what they were looking for in an old motion picture of the Tarzan series.

With all this the matter should have ended, but some of the Nazis, being a thorough and suspicious lot, kept it alive in a prolonged interchange of instructions, questions, and replies. Formally and technically conceding that no one had deserted from the *Schleswig-Holstein*, they nevertheless demanded to know what had become of the deserter, and they handled truth altogether as an instrument so flexible that it was bound to turn upon itself. The confidential files became larger and larger. Not only did the right hand not know what the left hand was intimating, but the right hand no longer knew about the right hand, and the left hand about the left. There was some reason to believe that the affair was even discussed at Berchtesgaden, but without that clarity which might have led to some determination of the issue.

However that may have been, when the guns of the

Schleswig-Holstein fired into Danzig on the fateful day of the new war Hugo Becker was not on board. He could not have been, for he was standing on the red earth of the high veld, and his wife was with him.

30